GOIN...

Three pounced at once. He stopped one with a straight arm to the mouth, another with a jolt to the gut, the third by kicking him in the knee, and when the cowboy doubled over, kneed him in the face.

"He fights dirty!" one shouted.

"Pound the son of a bitch!" another urged.

Everything became a blur of fists and arms and faces furious with bloodlust.

Fargo was a tornado. Blocking, weaving, dodging, punching, he more than held his own.

A chair crashed to the floor. A table was tipped over. Two more punchers were sprawled on the floor and Fargo tilted another onto his toes and cocked an arm to stretch him out, too.

Suddenly the back of his head exploded with pain. A wave of darkness swallowed him and he was vaguely aware of the floor rushing up to meet his face. . . .

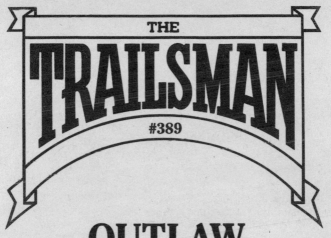

THE TRAILSMAN

#389

OUTLAW TRACKDOWN

by

Jon Sharpe

A SIGNET BOOK

SIGNET
Published by the Penguin Group
Penguin Group (USA) LLC, 375 Hudson Street,
New York, New York 10014

USA I Canada I UK I Ireland I Australia I New Zealand I India I South Africa I China
penguin.com
A Penguin Random House Company

First published by Signet, an imprint of New American Library,
a division of Penguin Group (USA) LLC

First Printing, March 2014

The first chapter of this book previously appeared in *Borderland Bloodbath*, the three
hundred eighty-eighth volume in this series.

 REGISTERED TRADEMARK—MARCA REGISTRADA

ISBN 978-0-451-46721-8

Printed in the United States of America
10 9 8 7 6 5 4 3 2 1

The Trailsman

Beginnings . . . they bend the tree and they mark the man. Skye Fargo was born when he was eighteen. Terror was his midwife, vengeance his first cry. Killing spawned Skye Fargo, ruthless, cold-blooded murder. Out of the acrid smoke of gunpowder still hanging in the air, he rose, cried out a promise never forgotten.

The Trailsman they began to call him all across the West: searcher, scout, hunter, the man who could see where others only looked, his skills for hire but not his soul, the man who lived each day to the fullest, yet trailed each tomorrow. Skye Fargo, the Trailsman, the seeker who could take the wildness of a land and the wanting of a woman and make them his own.

Wyoming, 1861—where a young killer has gone on a spree and has Fargo in his gun sights.

1

It isn't every day a man starts a brawl.

Skye Fargo had no intention of starting one when he stopped at the saloon in a sleepy little town called Horse Creek. He had a full poke after being paid for a scouting hitch with the army and figured to treat himself to a bottle of Monongahela, a card game, and a willing dove, not necessarily in that order.

So when he ambled into a whiskey mill called The Tumbleweed he wasn't looking for trouble. He was looking for a good time.

Fargo strode to the bar and smacked it for service. Not that he need have bothered. Other than an old-timer sucking down bug juice like it was the elixir of life, the only other patrons were three townsmen playing cards.

The bartender waddled over and asked, "What'll it be, mister?"

Fargo told him and fished a coin from his poke and plunked it down. "Quiet little town you have here."

The bartender had turned to a shelf, and grunted.

"What do you do for excitement? Watch the grass grow?"

"Haven't heard that one before," the bartender said.

"Had much Indian trouble hereabouts?" Fargo wondered. The Cheyenne had been acting up recently. They'd had their fill of the white invasion and were raiding homesteads and attacking stagecoaches.

"Doesn't everybody?" was the barman's response.

"I'm not asking everybody," Fargo said. "I'm asking you."

The bartender selected a glass from a pile next to a dirty cloth and picked up the dirty cloth and wiped it. "Our problem ain't Injuns. It's outlaws. They've hit three farms in the past couple of months and struck the Overland stage and got away with the money box." He set the glass on the bar and turned and chose a bottle.

Fargo picked up the glass. "You call this clean?" He wasn't fussy but there was . . . something . . . crusted a quarter-inch thick on the bottom, and a few brown smudges besides.

"I just wiped it. You saw me."

"It would be cleaner if I wiped it with my ass."

"Here now," the barkeep said indignantly. "You're not funny."

"Do you see me laughing?"

The man looked at Fargo and opened his mouth to say something but seemed to think better of it and held out his hand. "Give it to me. I'll wash it."

Fargo watched him dip it in a bucket of dirty water and then dry it with the dirty cloth. "You're something," he said.

"How's that again?"

"Forget the glass. I'll buy a bottle. One that hasn't been opened."

"First you want a clean glass and now you want a bottle," the bartender grumbled. "I wish you'd make up your mind."

"I just did."

Fargo's tone caused the barman to stiffen. "I don't want no trouble. I'm just doing my job."

"A goat could do it better."

Turning to a shelf lined with bottles, the barkeep muttered, "You have no call to insult me."

"The bottle," Fargo said. "This year."

"Damn, you are prickly."

Fargo snatched the bottle and opened it himself and tilted it to his mouth. The burning sensation brought a welcome warmth and he could feel himself relax.

"Happy now?"

Just then the batwings creaked and in came half a dozen cowboys. Smiling and joshing one another, they strolled to the bar.

One of them bumped Fargo with his shoulder and went on talking to his pard. About to take a swallow, Fargo felt his arm jostled a second time and whiskey spilled onto his chin.

". . . heard that calf when we branded it," the cow nurse was saying. "It screamed just like a female, I swear."

"Peckerwood," Fargo said, and jabbed the puncher with his elbow so hard, it rocked the cowboy onto his bootheels.

"What the hell was that for?" the cowboy demanded, growing red in the face.

"You know damn well." Fargo sleeved his chin with his buckskins. "Bump me again and I'll lay you out."

"I'd like to see you try."

Fargo should have let it go. That's what anyone with a lick of common sense would do. But the cowpoke's smug smirk was like a slap to the face. Then there was the unwritten law that you never, ever jostled a man taking a drink. "I believe I will," he said, and swung.

2

2

Fargo nearly always held a bottle or a glass in his left hand. He liked to keep his right hand free in case he had to resort to his Colt. Or, in this instance, his fist. He caught the cowpoke flush on the chin and sent him tottering against the others.

They squawked and cursed and caught their friend as he fell, and then held him and glared while he shook his head to clear it.

"Here now," growled a tall drink of water in a high-crowned hat. "What's this about, Floyd?"

"He hit me," Floyd said.

"How come?"

"Damned if I know."

"Liar," Fargo said.

The tall one glanced at the barkeep. "What about it, Harvey? Why'd this Daniel Boone hit Floyd?"

Harvey grinned wickedly at Fargo and said with a straight face, "He's half-drunk and on the prod."

"I'll show you prod," Fargo said, and hit the barkeep on the side of the head with the bottle. It shattered and Harvey screeched and clutched at his ear.

"Get him, boys!" the tall puncher hollered.

And just like that, Fargo was in cowboys up to his armpits. They came in a rush, cursing and swinging wildly, nearly tripping over one another in their eagerness. If they'd had the brains to surround him, the fight would have been over then and there. But they didn't, enabling him to skip out of reach and move wide of the bar so he had plenty of room.

"I've got him!" a cowpoke cried, and let loose with what he must have reckoned was a haymaker.

Fargo ducked, countered with a left uppercut and a right cross, and had the satisfaction of seeing the cowhand go down like a poled ox. But there were still five left and they were plenty mad. Three pounced at once. He stopped one with a straight arm to the

3

mouth, another with a jolt to the gut, the third by kicking him in the knee, and when the cowboy doubled over, kneed him in the face.

"He fights dirty!" one shouted.

"Pound the son of a bitch!" another urged.

Everything became a blur of fists and arms and faces furious with bloodlust.

Fargo was a tornado. Blocking, weaving, dodging, punching, he more than held his own.

A chair crashed to the floor. A table was tipped over. Two more punchers were sprawled on the floor and Fargo tilted another onto his toes and cocked an arm to stretch him out, too.

Suddenly the back of his head exploded with pain. A wave of darkness swallowed him and he was vaguely aware of the floor rushing up to meet his face.

The next thing Fargo knew, someone was whistling. He heard it as if from the end of a tunnel. A pale light appeared and he climbed toward it and grimaced when his eyes blinked open.

He was on his back on a cot in a jail cell. The cot had a musty smell and the cell was in shadow save for a shaft of sunlight split by the bars in a small window.

The whistler was over at a desk, his boots propped up, a tin star pinned to his shirt.

Fargo raised his head and gingerly felt the goose egg that had sprouted. His hat was on the floor and he slowly sat up, carefully jammed it on, and stood. For a few seconds the cell swayed. Or he did. "You didn't have to hit me so hard."

The man at the desk jumped as if he'd been pricked with a knife. His boots smacked down and he rose and ambled over, grinning. He wasn't much over twenty, with hair the color of corn, and freckles, no less. "Heck, mister. It weren't me that clubbed you. It was the marshal."

Fargo moved to the bars. "How long have I been in here?"

"Not long at all. Wasn't twenty minutes ago that those cowpokes from the Lazy J carted you in. The marshal made them do it and gave them a talkin' to about disturbin' the peace and fined them each ten dollars. They weren't happy about that, let me tell you."

"Why aren't they in here with me?"

"Harvey over at the saloon told the marshal that you were the troublemaker, not them."

"As soon as I'm out, I'll go have a talk with Harvey," Fargo promised himself.

"You'd best behave if you know what's good for you." The freckles shifted as the man smiled. "I'm Deputy Wilkins, by the way. Pleased to meet you."

Fargo squinted and saw that he was serious. "Who is this marshal you keep jabbering about?"

"Marshal Coltraine," Deputy Wilkins declared with considerable pride. "Luther Coltraine. Could be you've heard of him."

Fargo had, in fact. Coltraine was considered one of the best. A Texan, he'd tamed the town of Brazos, the most violent nest of hard cases on the border, some said. Other towns, too. But all of them in Texas. "What is Luther Coltraine doing way up here in Wyoming Territory?" Or so some were calling it even though the legislature hadn't gotten around to making it official yet.

"Why wouldn't he be? Our town needs a lawman like everywhere else."

"When do I get out?"

"That's not up to me," Deputy Wilkins said. "You have to ask the marshal."

Fargo gazed at the otherwise empty office. "And where might he be?"

"Probably off visitin' his gal." Deputy Wilkins lowered his voice as if afraid of being overheard. "Between you and me, he's taken a powerful likin' to a certain young filly."

"You don't say." Fargo had no hankering to stay behind bars any longer than he had to. "Why don't you fetch him so I can pay my fine and get out of here."

"I couldn't do that."

"Why not?"

"Bother the marshal when he's courtin'? That'd hardly be polite." Deputy Wilkins grinned. "Would you like somethin' to eat instead? I have some crackers. And I've got prune juice to wash 'em down."

"You are a marvel," Fargo said. "But no, thanks."

"The prune juice is fresh. My ma made it for me. She says that nothin' cleans a man out like prunes."

"Any chance I could have some whiskey?"

"You're joshin', right?"

"I was afraid of that." Fargo sighed and moved to the cot and sat. "The marshal shouldn't be gone more than an hour or so,"

Deputy Wilkins said. "He does his serious courtin' at night and right now it's the middle of the day."

"Just a glass," Fargo said. "Half full."

"No and no. I never yet heard of a jail that gives its prisoners whiskey."

"Too bad," Fargo said. His head was pounding like a blacksmith's hammer. "It would help dull the pain."

"You're hurtin'?"

"It wasn't a love tap your marshal gave me," Fargo informed him, and closed his eyes. He figured he might as well catch up on his rest since he couldn't do anything else.

"I hate it when folks hurt," Deputy Wilkins said. "My ma always says that when people hurt, you should help them."

"Does she, now?" Fargo responded, wishing the deputy would go away so he could sleep.

"You know what? If I give you some, do you give me your word you won't tell the marshal?"

From behind Deputy Wilkins came a growled, "Tell me what?"

3

Deputy Wilkins jumped so high, it was a wonder he didn't hit the ceiling. Fargo almost laughed but then he got a good look at the man behind Wilkins and he sobered right quick.

Some lawmen didn't look the part. Wilkins, for one. Once Fargo met a sheriff who resembled a plump turkey. Another time, it was a pasty pastry roll who would have been content to sit in his office day in and day out, stuffing his face with sweets.

Marshal Luther Coltraine looked the part. He was tall, even taller than Fargo, and his shoulders were just as wide. He had a powerful chest any man would envy, and a face that looked as if it had been chiseled from granite. His eyes were a striking green. On his hip was a pearl-handled Smith & Wesson. His badge was pinned to a black leather vest that matched his black hat.

"Marshal!" Deputy Wilkins bleated.

"I asked you a question," Coltraine said with as thick a Texas drawl as Fargo ever heard. "What were you fixin' to give the prisoner?"

Wilkins coughed and fidgeted and said barely loud enough to hear, "Whiskey."

Coltraine's jaw muscles twitched. "What's my rule?"

"No liquor, ever," Deputy Wilkins said, and went on in a rush, "But it's for medicinal purposes. He's got a lump on his head from that wallop you gave him."

"And you figure to get him so drunk he won't feel the pain?"

"No, sir," Wilkins said quickly. "I was only goin' to give him half a glass."

"Not if you like your job, you're not. Don't ever let a prisoner talk you into doin' somethin' you shouldn't." Marshal Coltraine strode to the cell and Wilkins couldn't skip aside fast enough. "What do you have to say for yourself, mister?"

"I want out," Fargo said.

"I bet you do. But that's not goin' to happen until I say it is."

"I'm a scout . . ." Fargo began.

"I figured as much, how you're dressed. So what?"

"So I just came from Fort Laramie and was minding my own business when those cow nurses jumped me."

"That's not how they tell it, and the barkeep backs their story. Harvey says you were lookin' for trouble from the moment you walked in."

"Harvey will have some trouble of his own once I'm out," Fargo vowed a second time.

"Talk like that will keep you in here for a month of Sundays."

"Damn it, Marshal . . ."

Coltraine held up a big hand. "Cussin' me won't help your cause any, either. You're too hotheaded for your own good."

Fargo bit off a sharp retort. He might as well face the fact that unless he did as the lawman wanted, he'd be lucky to get out before Christmas.

"What's your handle?"

Fargo told him.

The marshal looked him up and down and said, "Heard of you. They say you're one of the best trackers alive."

"I've had some practice," Fargo said.

"I also hear tell you've had a lot of practice drinkin' and playin' cards and dallyin' with doves."

Fargo was sure he caught the hint of a grin, which was encouraging. "I admit I am fond of dallying."

Coltraine chuckled. "I've done a bit of it my own self."

"You've done what now, Marshal?" Deputy Wilkins asked.

Coltraine glanced at him as if he'd forgotten he was there. "Go to the general store and buy us some coffee. We're plumb out."

"Coffee? At this time of day? Usually you have it in the mornin'."

"Our guest here will need some to clear his head."

Deputy Wilkins scratched his. "I must have missed somethin'. When did he go from prisoner to guest?"

"When I say he did. Now scat."

Thoroughly confused, the deputy and his freckles departed in a hurry. As he went out he said, "I'll be back in two shakes of a lamb's tail."

Marshal Coltraine sighed. "He's next to worthless but he's the only one who applied for the job so I'm stuck with him."

"If you don't mind my saying," Fargo said, "this seems a strange place to find a man of your caliber."

"What a nice thing to say," Coltraine said, genuinely flattered. "They offered it to me and I took it. But you're right. Horse Creek ain't Texas. Most days it's so peaceful, you'd swear you can hear the dust blow down the street."

"And you like it that way?" Fargo asked in mild surprise. Accounts had it that Coltraine was a real fire-breather who thrived on living on the razor's edge. The sort of hombre who would walk into danger without batting an eye.

Coltraine shrugged. "It's a living." He turned and stepped to a peg on the wall and grabbed a large key ring with only one key. Inserting the key into the cell door, he twisted, and at the loud click, pulled the door wide. "Come out and have a seat."

Fargo was glad to. He figured the lawman was about to let him go. "Do I owe the saloon anything for damages?"

"Nothin' was busted, so no. But there's a forty dollar fine for disturbin' the peace," Coltraine said.

"The cowboys only had to pay ten."

"Answer me true. Did you take the first swing or did they?"

Fargo didn't hesitate. "Me."

"Then it's forty dollars and be thankful I don't want more."

"Don't I go up before a judge first?"

"The judge is off fishin'. I'll collect it for him and you can leave inside the hour."

"Why wait that long?" Fargo wanted to climb on the Ovaro and light a shuck.

Coltraine sat at his desk, opened a bottom drawer, and took out a half-empty bottle of whiskey. He set it in front of him and said, "Interested?"

"I thought you sent freckles for coffee?"

"That or this," Coltraine said. "Your choice."

"It's no choice at all," Fargo said, and grinned.

Coltraine produced a glass and poured three fingers worth and skid it across. "This will clear your head a lot faster than coffee."

"I'm obliged." Fargo tossed it off and winced at a spike of pain. "How hard did you hit me, anyhow?"

"It was a good rap. A fella gets the knack for pistol-whippin' after he's worn a badge for a spell." Coltraine didn't bother with the glass. He savored a long swig and let out a contented sigh. "Nothin' better for washin' down the dust." He returned the bottle and the glass to the bottom drawer and closed the drawer.

"So I can go?"

"You're forgettin' the forty dollars."

Fargo reached for his poke, and froze. It wasn't there. He groped his buckskins and exploded with an oath.

"Lookin' for this?" Coltraine reached under his vest.

Fargo hefted it. He would swear it was lighter than it had been when he paid for his bottle in the saloon. Undoing the tie string, he fished inside. He wasn't about to come right out and accuse the lawman of helping himself, but if he had to guess without looking, he'd say a double eagle and some other coins were missing.

As if he sensed what Fargo was thinking, Coltraine said, "That's what was in it when I took it off you."

Fargo wondered if one of the cowboys could have palmed a few coins before the lawman carted him off. But if that was the case, why hadn't the puncher taken the whole poke?

"As soon as you pay you can be on your way," Coltraine told him. "No goin' back to the saloon, though. No goin' anywhere except out of town."

"Fine by me."

"Don't take it personal. Those cowhands are still in town and seein' you might stir them up." The lawman spread his big hands on the desk. "I like a quiet town, Fargo. As quiet as can be."

Just then Horse Creek rocked to the blasts of gunfire.

4

"What the hell?" Marshal Luther Coltraine blurted as more gun-shots boomed.

Fargo was already out of his chair. He was turning toward the door when he realized that, in the first place, it was the marshal's business, and in the second, he didn't have his Colt.

Somewhere a woman screamed.

Coltraine still sat there as if in shock.

"You might want to see what the ruckus is about," Fargo said.

The lawman pushed to his feet and came around the desk. He was halfway to the front door when it burst open and in spilled Deputy Wilkins looking stricken and out of breath.

"Marshal! Marshal! The bank is bein' robbed. It's the Cotton brothers and those others!"

Coltraine stared out the door but didn't move until another scream galvanized him into drawing his Smith & Wesson and hur-rying out. Wilkins dogged him like a puppy.

Fargo moved to the window.

Up and down the street, panic reigned. People scurried every which way. Two bodies lay sprawled in spreading pools of scarlet.

About a block and a half away stood the Horse Creek bank. Fargo had to crane his neck to see it. A frame wood building like all the rest, it had a hitch rail out front. Four horses were next to it but hadn't been tied off. On two other mounts were men with pis-tols, one facing up the street, one down it. Even as Fargo looked, the man facing his way pointed his six-shooter and fired at a store owner who had appeared holding a shotgun. The owner grabbed at his chest and toppled.

The two outlaws on horseback were holding the good citizens of Horse Creek at bay while their pards robbed the bank.

Marshal Coltraine raised his Smith & Wesson but the same out-law spotted him and snapped a shot and Coltraine ducked behind a water barrel. Deputy Wilkins stuck to him like glue.

That was when the four outlaws who had gone into the bank

rushed out again. Two carried burlap bags. A third had a rifle and he began spraying lead at anything that moved.

The last was the youngest. He had a six-gun in one hand and was pulling a woman after him. She fought, trying to break free, but couldn't stop him from hauling her to a horse. He barked something at the man with the rifle and together they seized her and flung her up.

"Amanda!" Deputy Wilkins cried. He started to stand but Marshal Coltraine yanked him down just as the outlaw facing that end of the street snapped a shot at them.

A townsman charged out of a house and commenced to fire a rifle like a madman. He got off four or five shots before the outlaw shot him in the head.

The rest scrambled to mount. A horse spooked by the din kept shying. The outlaw trying to climb on got hold of the saddle horn but couldn't swing up.

The young one shouted at him, and gestured, and the young one and the other five took off up the street.

In sudden desperation the last outlaw managed to clamber on and reined after them.

Marshal Coltraine stepped into the open and took deliberate aim. He had a clear shot but he didn't shoot. Instead, Coltraine scowled and jerked his revolver down.

To the thunder of hooves, the outlaws fled

Only when the hoofbeats faded and silence fell did Horse Creek stir. People came out of buildings and from behind corners and gazed about in disbelief. A woman broke into tears.

Fargo went outside. The lawman hadn't moved and the deputy was fidgeting like a hound dog eager to take up the scene.

"Marshal?" Wilkins said. "Marshal?"

Coltraine shoved the Smith & Wesson into his holster and moved toward the bank.

An elderly woman hurried to the body of an elderly man and sank to her knees and let out a wail.

Fargo drifted down the street with a lot of others. Many were in a daze. One man kept saying over and over, "Did you see that? Did you see that?"

Marshal Coltraine was almost to the bank when a portly man in a suit stumbled out. He was bald and his pate glistened red from a gash above his ear. He had a hand to the wound and clutched at the empty air with the other as if for support. Coltraine caught him before he could fall.

"It was the Cotton Gang," someone exclaimed.

"They rode in as brazen as anything," said someone else.

"That Hoby Cotton," said yet another, "taking Amanda Brenner with them like he done."

"We'll hang him," declared a fourth. "Him and that whole wild bunch, and good riddance."

The portly man had gripped Coltraine's shirt. "They took her! They took my daughter!"

"I saw, Mr. Brenner," Coltraine said.

"What are you waiting for? Go after them. They can't have gotten far. You have to save her. Do you hear me? Save her!" That last was a near-hysterical appeal that ended with a gasp as the portly man passed out.

A townsman carrying a black medical bag ran up.

The marshal and his deputy entered the bank and not half a minute later Wilkins reappeared supporting a middle-aged woman so shaken, she couldn't walk unaided. He steered her toward the marshal's office. As they went past Fargo, Deputy Wilkins glanced at him and sadly shook his head.

Fargo spied the cowboys he had clashed with over in front of the saloon. They paid him no mind. A couple of the punchers had unlimbered their six-shooters during the fracas but hadn't used them.

Marshal Coltraine came out of the bank looking mad enough to kill. "They shot the teller, Ed Zeigler," he said to the doctor, who was tending to Brenner.

"I'll see to him next," the sawbones said.

"No need," Coltraine said. "His brains are splattered all over the teller's cage." He paused. "How bad is Mr. Brenner?"

"He was struck over the head," the doctor said. "Beyond that, I won't know until I get him to my office and examine him."

Coltraine moved from body to body, making sure they were beyond help, then strode over to Fargo. "Come with me."

"So much for peace and quiet," Fargo said, falling into step beside him.

"If that was a joke it was in poor taste."

"I'd like to pay the forty dollars and be on my way."

"Was that another joke?"

"You're fixing to rustle up a posse and go after them," Fargo figured. "I don't want to be stuck here until you get back."

"You won't be," Coltraine said. They reached the office and he stopped and stared up the street in the direction the outlaws had gone. "When I go after them, you're comin' with me."

5

"How's that again?" Fargo said.

The marshal ignored him and went in.

In a chair by the desk the middle-aged woman shook and sniffled. Deputy Wilkins was patting her lightly on the shoulder and saying, "There, there, Mabel. There, there."

Coltraine motioned for Wilkins to move aside and squatted next to the chair. Clasping one of the woman's hands in his, he said gently, "Mabel? I need to ask you some questions. Are you able?"

Mabel sniffled some more, and nodded. "It was horrible. Just horrible. They barged in, shouting and waving their guns."

"Tell me everything," the lawman said. "What they did. What they said."

"I was at my desk preparing a letter Mr. Brenner needs to send to Cheyenne when that awful Hoby Cotton and his brothers and that Timbre fellow with the scar stormed right in. Mr. Brenner was in his office with Amanda and came out and demanded to know what the uproar was about. And do you know what Hoby Cotton did?"

"I wasn't there," Coltraine said.

"He shot poor Ed Zeigler in the head and laughed and said that Mr. Brenner should guess." Mabel dabbed at her nose with a sleeve and the marshal took a folded handkerchief from a pocket and gave it to her.

"When you can, go on."

Mabel nodded. She blew her nose and said, "Sorry," and crumpled the handkerchief in her lap. "Anyway, Mr. Brenner moved toward Ed, and Hoby Cotton hit him with his six-shooter. Then Hoby shook him and told him to open the safe but Mr. Brenner refused. Even with blood streaming down his head, Mr. Brenner looked that ruffian right in the eye and refused."

"Brenner was lucky Cotton didn't shoot him."

"Hoby almost did. But then Amanda came running, yelling at

him to leave her father alone. And do you know what that monster did next?"

Coltraine waited.

"He grabbed Amanda and shoved his gun in her face and told Mr. Brenner that if he didn't open the safe, he'd do to her as he'd just done to Ed."

"So Brenner opened the safe."

"What else could he do?" Mabel said. "See his daughter gunned down in front of his very eyes?" She shed more tears and sniffled. "Mr. Brenner went to the safe and opened it. He had to do it quickly, too, because Hoby had pulled back the hammer on his revolver and was saying as he'd by-God do it if Brenner didn't move faster."

"How much did they get?"

"I don't know. Only Mr. Brenner would," Mabel answered. "They stuffed some burlap sacks with everything from the safe and the teller's drawer and even rifled my drawers looking for more. Then that Timbre, who was looking out the door the whole time, said as how he saw you and the deputy and that people were coming from all over and they'd best fan the breeze. And they left."

"Did the others say anything? Hoby's brothers, for instance?"

"I didn't pay much attention to them. It was Hoby Cotton I was watching."

"Think, Mabel," Coltraine urged. "It's important. They might have let drop some clue to where they're headed."

"I don't recall a word about that," Mabel said. "And if you head right out after them, you won't need a clue. All you'll need is a good tracker."

"I've already thought of that," Coltraine said, and looked over at Fargo.

"Hell," Fargo said.

Coltraine squeezed Mabel's hand and stood. "Deputy Wilkins will take you back to the bank. Do what you can to get me a tally on how much they stole."

"Why is that so important?"

"It just is." Coltraine eased her out of the chair and guided her to the door, where Deputy Wilkins took over and escorted her from the office.

"I have to attend to the bodies and go talk to the banker," Coltraine said. "Stay put until I get back."

"Hold on," Fargo said. "I didn't volunteer to track for you."

"You're doin' it whether you want to or not."

"You can't force me."

"You did see them take the girl? She's only eighteen. And you know what they'll do to her."

Fargo frowned. "She's the only reason I'd agree. But I'd like to be asked."

"Fair enough. I'm askin'. But you still have to pay your fine." Coltraine opened the door. "Your Colt is in the middle drawer on the left. We leave in half an hour."

"The sooner, the better. Every minute you waste . . . "

"I know," Coltraine said gruffly, and was gone.

Fargo reclaimed his Colt and made sure five pills were in the wheel. He spun it a few times and twirled it into his holster and patted it. Going out, he watched as a buckboard rattled around a corner and several men prepared to load the bodies.

A pall of gloom had settled over the town and every face was either downcast or stamped with fury.

Deputy Wilkins returned and asked where the marshal had gotten to. "This is terrible, just terrible," he remarked. "Amanda is the sweetest gal anywhere. If that Hoby Cotton touches her . . ." He stopped and balled his fists.

"There were six of them," Fargo said.

Wilkins absently nodded while watching a body being lifted. "Hoby Cotton and his brothers, Granger and Semple. Then there's Timbre Wilson, Abe Foreman, and Rufus Holloway."

"You know all their names?"

"I should. They've been terrorizin' the territory for goin' on half a year now. They're snake mean, every mother's son. That Hoby is the worst. He's killed four men that the marshal and me know of."

"Why isn't he behind bars or been hung?"

"You think the marshal hasn't tried to catch him?" Wilkins said. "Must be fifty times or more we've gotten a tip on where they are and it's always the same. They're gone when we get there."

"Fifty times is a lot."

"Maybe it was only forty. The thing is, they never make camp in the same place twice. They're always on the move. And they have more hideouts than you have fingers and toes."

"Have you tried a tracker?"

Wilkins nodded. "Jonas over to the general store did some when he was younger but he hasn't been of much use. We used an old hound once that belongs to a farmer but all the dog did was sniff a lot and run in circles."

"I guess that tells me why the marshal wants me to go along."

"He does?" Deputy Wilkins seemed to grow concerned. "Listen to me, mister. I don't know you from Adam but if you're helpin' us then you deserve to know. Those men are hard cases."

"I reckoned as much."

"You have to be careful. If they find out you're after them, they're liable to turn on you. They've done it before. One time the marshal went out with seven men and he was the only one who made it back."

"I don't die easy," Fargo said.

"I hope not," Deputy Wilkins said earnestly, "for your sake."

6

Fargo was tired of waiting. Over an hour had gone by and the marshal hadn't returned. With every wasted minute the outlaws and their captive got farther away. Were he the marshal, Fargo would have headed out after them just as soon as he could assemble a posse.

Coltraine finally appeared, strolling down the street as if he had all the time in the world. He stopped to talk to two women and then stopped to talk to several men. When he reached the jail he stopped yet again to take off his hat and run his fingers through his hair.

"Took you long enough," Fargo said as the door opened.

"I had a lot to do."

"The Cottons and their friends could be in Nebraska Territory by now."

Coltraine had stepped to a rifle rack. "I don't need your guff. I've worn a tin star for pretty near fifteen years now. I know my job better than you."

Fargo decided to drop it. "How many did you line up for the posse besides me?"

"Wilkins," Coltraine said, bringing a Spencer over to the desk, "and nine others. They're to meet here at the bottom of the hour."

"That's another twenty minutes."

"So?" Coltraine proceeded to methodically load the Spencer.

"I'll fetch my horse and be back," Fargo said, and turned to leave.

"Not so fast. You're forgettin' somethin'." Coltraine held out a palm. "The forty dollars."

"That's all you can think of at a time like this?"

"A fine is a fine and collectin' them is my job."

Simmering, Fargo produced his poke and counted out the forty. "Happy now?"

"Pleased as punch." Coltraine hefted the coins and smiled. "The town of Horse Creek thanks you."

"I want a receipt."

"See me after we get back." Coltraine resumed loading, and when Fargo didn't move, looked up. "Anything else?"

"No." Fargo got out of there before he said something Coltraine would resent.

Deputy Wilkins was just coming out of the stable, leading a sorrel. He saw Fargo and waved.

Fargo was tempted to go into the saloon. Instead he unwrapped the Ovaro's reins from the hitch rail and led the stallion to the marshal's.

More waiting added to his annoyance. It was a full half an hour before the marshal emerged. By then three townsmen had shown up leading their mounts. All wore store-bought duds and looked about as fearsome as kittens.

"Are you with the posse too?" asked a pudgy man in a bowler who was sweating buckets.

Fargo nodded.

"I don't believe I've seen you before. I'm Norman. I work as a clerk over to the Emporium."

Fargo noticed that the holster strapped around Norman's thick waist had a lot of dust on it. "Use that much?"

Norman touched his six-gun as if surprised it was there. "Mercy, no. Didn't you hear me say I'm a clerk? I got this years ago but haven't used it once."

"Yet you offered to join the posse."

"Offered, nothing," Norman said. "The marshal came into the Emporium and told me I'm coming along."

"Why you? Are you good on horseback?"

Norman stared at his horse as if it were from another planet. "Not really, no. I rode some when I was a boy but to tell the truth, horses have always scared me."

"Scared you how?"

Norman swallowed. "It's those big teeth. I can't help imagining what would happen if one took a bite out of me. And then there's those hooves. Why, a horse's hoof can crush a man's skull."

Fargo turned to the second townsman. "How about you? Can you ride and shoot?"

This one was older and had stubble on his chin and a perpetual scowl. "Sure I can ride. I work at the stable. Not that that gave the marshal any call to come marching in and say I was going with the posse and be ready, or else."

"How are you with that six-gun you're wearing?" Fargo asked.

"I can hit a barn pretty good."

Fargo looked at the third townsman, who brought to mind a mouse in a cheap suit. "Let me guess. You're hell on wheels with a six-shooter and a horse."

The mouse grinned. "Would that I were. I wouldn't be an accountant. I'd be a lawman like the marshal."

"This will be some posse," Fargo said.

"Don't worry," Norman said. "We might not be much but they are." And he gestured.

The cowboys Fargo had tangled with appeared a little the worse for tangling. Nearly all had bruises and one puncher's nose was swollen.

"Why, look at them," the townsman who was afraid of horses said. "They look as if they've been in a fight."

"That's cowpokes for you," Norman said. "Always drinking and fighting and trifling with women."

The cowhand called Floyd came to a stop and the rest followed suit. Hooking his thumbs in his gun belt, he regarded Fargo as if Fargo were a bug he'd like to squash. "Look who it is, boys."

The tall cowboy in the high-crowned hat surprised Fargo by smiling. "You're one tough hombre, mister. I haven't been hit so hard since I was knee high to a calf and my grandpa walloped me for lyin'."

"A person should never lie, Mr. Rollins," Norman said. "It's not nice."

"It's just Rollins," the tall cowboy said. "And why are you here? You couldn't lick a puppy if the pup was blindfolded."

Fargo chuckled.

Norman drew himself up. "I might not be much account as a fighter but I remember prices really good."

"How much for outlaws these days?" Rollins asked.

Several cowboys—and Fargo—laughed.

"Quit picking on Norman," the stableman said. "Everybody knows he's as nice as can be."

"A posse is no place for nice," Rollins said.

"I must be of some use or the marshal wouldn't have picked me," Norman declared. "Although I confess that for the life of me I can't imagine what use that could be."

Floyd continued to glare at Fargo. "This ain't over between us, mister. Not by a long shot."

"Don't mind him," Rollins said. "You cracked a tooth when you slugged him and now he has to go to the dentist and he hates dentists."

"I like my dentist," Norman said. "He always gives me a piece of hard candy when he's done."

"Shut up, you infant," Floyd snapped.

Just then the door opened and out strolled Marshal Coltraine, the Spencer in the crook of his elbow. "I see all of you have met. You know why you're here so let's get to it." He paused. "Anyone have anything to say before we head out?"

"This is some posse," Fargo said.

7

The Cotton Gang, it was called, had headed east but only for half a mile. At that point they circled to the northwest and the distant Laramie Mountains.

"They must have figured to throw us off their scent," the stableman remarked.

"I doubt that," Marshal Coltraine said.

So did Fargo. The tracks were plain as could be. He was out in front, where Coltraine wanted him. They hadn't spoken two words since they left Horse Creek but now the marshal brought his bay alongside the Ovaro.

"So far, so good."

"We've hardly started," Fargo said.

The rolling grassland was dotted with mesquite and, now and then, stands of oak. Here and there ribbons of cottonwoods grew along small creeks, tributaries of Horse Creek itself.

"With any luck we'll catch up to them by nightfall," Coltraine predicted.

Fargo doubted, that, too. Not at the snail's pace Coltraine had set. They were to hold their horses to a walk so as not to tire them. "It would help if we went faster," he mentioned.

"I know what I'm doing."

"You keep saying that."

Coltraine frowned. "The best horse of this bunch is yours. It could go all day and all night, and so could mine if it came to that but it's not as used to hard travel as yours and would be worn out by mornin'. Those cowhands have good mounts but they rode them hard to town and the horses could use some rest. Norman and Scully and Burt have animals that aren't worth a damn. Wilkins's horse isn't much better. So if I push hard, by sunset the only ones who could still go on would be you and me."

"About those townsmen you picked . . ."

"They're all bachelors. No wives, no kids. And believe it or not, there aren't a lot of single gents in Horse Creek. Most are family men, and I wasn't about to ask a husband and father to go after some of the worst killers in the territory."

"I'll be damned," Fargo said, and grinned. "You do know what you're doing."

"We're takin' our sweet time so our horses will have some wind left when we catch up, and to give those who don't have much grit to steady their nerves for the shootin'."

Fargo was impressed. He'd misjudged Coltraine completely. "Here I reckoned you were dragging your heels because you didn't want to tangle with the Cottons and their friends."

"I want nothin' more than to buck them out in gore," Coltraine replied. "But I have to do it smart. And I have to be extra careful because of Amanda Brenner. Any harm comes to that gal, I'll never forgive myself."

After that, Fargo did whatever the lawman asked without question. Along about four o'clock, as they neared the foothills, Coltraine asked him to go on ahead and make sure it was safe.

"It's a likely spot for an ambush. The Cottons could lie up there and pick us off, easy. Be careful."

The hills were mostly brown from the summer heat and sparse

with vegetation. A dry wash suggested to Fargo a way to wend in among them without being seen. The sides were high enough to hide the Ovaro but not him so he hunched low over the saddle horn.

Each hill he passed, he scanned from top to bottom. He saw no one, glimpsed no telltale flashes. When the wash veered away from the tracks he had been following, he reluctantly gigged the stallion up and out into the open.

He rode slowly, avoiding patches of rocky ground so the chink of horseshoes on stone wouldn't give him away.

The outlaws had slowed from a trot to a walk. Evidently they weren't worried about being pursued. Which was strange, given Luther Coltraine's reputation.

It was only a couple of hours to sunset and Fargo was almost in the shadow of the first mountain when he decided to go back and report that the outlaws showed no sign of stopping early.

Suddenly he heard voices. Startled, he drew rein and tilted his head to listen.

He wasn't imagining it. From not far ahead, the breeze brought a laugh and muffled talk.

Dismounting, Fargo yanked the Henry from the saddle scabbard and advanced on foot.

Between the last hill and a mountain grew an oasis of green. An acre or more of tall trees and undergrowth.

Unless Fargo was badly mistaken, there must be water. It explained why the outlaws had stopped so soon.

Common sense told him to ride back to the posse and bring Coltraine and the rest on as quickly as they could. But it would help if he could see the outlaw camp and maybe get some idea of how best to go about corralling them.

Girding himself, he broke into a sprint. He felt uneasy being so exposed but he reached cover without hearing a shout or a shot.

Sweat trickling down his back, Fargo crouched and crabbed forward. He saw the horses first, and a spring. Six horses, but only five outlaws. Nor was there any sign of the girl.

Fargo stopped in consternation. He wondered if he was too late, if the owlhoots had already had their way with her. But if so, where was she? Or her body?

Of the outlaws, Timbre Wilson was easy to peg. Someone in Horse Creek had mentioned a scar, and it was a doozy. A sword or a bowie had cleaved the left side of Wilson's face, splitting the cheek and just missing the eye. The scar ran from Wilson's jaw to his forehead. It lent his face a twisted, cruel aspect. He was squatting on his heels and the only one of the outlaws who didn't talk or smile.

Two others looked so much alike, they must be kin. Semple and Granger Cotton, Fargo reckoned. They were in their twenties, while their brother Hoby was supposed to be in his teens. Both sported sandy hair, worn long, and sandy beards, trimmed short.

Fargo had no idea how to tell Abe Foreman from Rufus Holloway. If he had to guess, he'd pick the one in homespun and whose beard fell to his waist as Rufus.

The bigger question, though, was where had Hoby Cotton gotten to? And where was the girl?

A horse moved and Fargo saw her lying on her side facing the spring. Her back was to him and her arms in front of her, so he didn't know if they were tied. Her legs weren't. Not that she would get far if she tried to run off with the outlaws so close.

Fargo had an inspiration. If he circled around, he could come up on her from the other side of the spring, catch her attention, and spirit her out of there. It was worth a try. Flattening, he crawled. Dry twigs that might snap and give him away, he moved aside. He avoided a jagged rock and deer droppings.

Soon he could hear what the outlaws were saying, and listened with half an ear as he went around a boulder.

". . . good haul. We have enough to last us the rest of the year if we don't go hog wild."

"Listen to you, Semple. Hog wild is all he knows. Remember Denver? We went there with five thousand in our saddlebags and he spent it inside of a week."

"Denver whores ain't cheap."

"Whores, hell. It was the gamblin' that did him in. It's the gamblin' that always does him in. He'd lose the shirt on his back if we let him."

Fargo knew they were talking about the missing Hoby. He found out where the youngest Cotton had gotten to when he raised his head to peer over a log and found himself staring into the barrel of a cocked revolver.

8

A round moon of a face popped above the log, a face with laughing eyes almost as blue as Fargo's own, and a mocking smile. A face as smooth as a baby's bottom save for peach fuzz on the chin. A face so boyish it belied the body it was attached to.

"Howdy, mister."

Fargo had frozen with that muzzle an inch from his nose. "Howdy, yourself," he said.

"What're you doin'?"

"Enjoying the day. You?"

The boy-man laughed. "Me, too. It tickled me seein' you sneak up on us. You're good at it."

"You're not bad yourself," Fargo said. "I didn't hear you come up on me."

"When it comes to sneaky, I'm the cat's meow."

"You'd be Hoby Cotton?"

Hoby bobbed his laughing moon face but his Colt stayed rock steady. "I'm plumb amazed sometimes at how many folks know me and I've never set eyes on them. Take you, for instance. We've never met. I'd recollect if we had. I have a good memory for faces."

"Skye Fargo," Fargo said.

"Sky what?"

"My name. Skye Fargo."

"Really? Your folks named you after the sky? Mine named me after my great grandpa on my ma's side."

"There's an 'e' on it."

"How's that again?"

"S-k-y-e," Fargo spelled it out for him.

"Well, now. That's too pretty to be a fella's name. You ought to be a girl." Hoby grinned. "As for spellin', I can't read or write a lick. Never learned how. My ma didn't believe in schoolin'."

"Your mother didn't think it might be good to know how to read?"

"She couldn't. She always said as how she didn't need no ABC's to get through life and we didn't, neither. We bein' me and my brothers yonder, Granger and Semple."

"You're from the South, I take it?" Fargo reckoned from his accent.

"Texas."

"There's a lot of that going around."

"I don't savvy."

"Marshal Luther Coltraine is from Texas. He's not far behind me with a posse."

"I know all about the great Luther Coltraine," Hoby said. "I'm guessin' he sent you on ahead to scout things out."

Fargo made a mental note not to underestimate this kid. Those laughing eyes hid a shrewd little monster. "You killed a man back in town."

"The teller," Hoby said. "I didn't like his ears. They were so big, it was a wonder they didn't flap when he moved."

"You shot him because of his ears?"

"Well, that, and I needed to scare the banker into openin' the safe. There's nothin' like splatterin' brains to scare folks."

"So what now?" Fargo asked. "You splatter mine?"

Hoby Cotton turned his head to the right and the left, inspecting Fargo's. "No, I like your ears. And I don't need to scare anybody at the moment."

"Thank you, God," Fargo said.

Laughing, Hoby rose while keeping him covered. "Suppose you let loose of that rifle and get to your feet with your hands in the air."

"Whatever you say."

"I like that," Hoby said.

"Like what?"

"I like to train folks to do whatever I want. My brothers, the others, they do what I tell 'em even though I'm the youngest because they know if they don't, I'll splatter their brains."

"You're big on splattering brains."

"The biggest."

Fargo set the Henry down and stood with his arms straight up. Part of him wanted to swat the boy's six-shooter and go for his own. He was quicker than most. But something—call it an instinct, a hunch, whatever—warned him that this killer with the laughing eyes might be his match.

"You listen real well," Hoby complimented him.

24

"I try."

"Keep it up and you'll live longer." Hoby turned his head without taking his blue eyes off Fargo and hollered, "Semple! Granger! The rest of you. Get the hell over here. We've got company."

There were shouts of surprise and the crash of underbrush, and in no time Fargo was surrounded by six hard cases with drawn six-guns.

"What have we here?" asked one of the older brothers.

"A fella with a girl's name," Hoby said. "I want you to watch him like a hawk, Granger." So saying, with dazzling speed he twirled his Colt into his holster.

"Want I should kill him?" Timbre Wilson asked.

"If I did I'd say so."

"He's with the posse, I bet," said the brother who must be Semple.

"Figured as much my own self," Hoby responded.

"What do you want to do with him if you don't want to kill him?" Timbre Wilson asked.

"Bring him along. We'll have coffee while I ponder on it some."

With the outlaws ringing him, Fargo was escorted out of the trees and over to the fire.

Amanda Brenner had sat up. Her brown hair was disheveled from the riding she'd done but otherwise she appeared unruffled by her ordeal. She hadn't been tied.

"Miss," Fargo said as he went by.

"Amanda sure is pretty, ain't she?" Hoby Cotton said.

"She has nice ears."

Hoby cackled and slapped his thigh. "That was a good one, mister. You have a knack for makin' me laugh."

"What's this about ears?" Granger asked.

"None of your beeswax." Hoby hunkered and commenced to fill a tin cup and offered it to Fargo. "Here. We don't have anything else but water if you'd rather have that."

"The coffee will do." Fargo was studying the others. They were wary of him but showed no inclination to do him harm, except for Timbre Wilson

"Now then," Hoby said, cupping a tin cup of his own. "Let's get to it. You're not from Horse Creek. Ain't a soul there wears buckskins. The way you move, how sneaky you are, I'm guessin' you're familiar with Injun ways."

"I hate redskins," Timbre Wilson said.

"You hate everybody," Hoby said.

"I'm a scout," Fargo revealed. He saw no reason not to.

"I hate scouts," Timbre Wilson said.

"You're itchin' to do him in, aren't you?" Hoby said.

Timbre Wilson pointed his pistol at Fargo's face. "Just say the word and it's done."

9

"I already told you no once," Hoby Cotton said, "and you know how I hate to repeat myself."

Timbre reluctantly lowered his six-shooter. "It's a mistake to let him go on breathin'."

"So now I'm dumb, am I?"

"You're the smartest gent I know," Timbre said. "Don't put words in my head that aren't there."

"And now you're tellin' me what to do."

"Damn it, Hoby," Timber said. "What's gotten into you? Since when do you take a stranger's side against your own pards?"

"I ain't against anybody. I just get tired of you bein' so cantankerous."

"You want me to leave, I will."

"No," Hoby said. "I keep you around because you're the one person in this world who likes to kill even more than me. My brothers only do it when they have to and Abe and Rufus hardly ever at all but you and me are killin' fiends."

"And damn proud of it," Timbre said.

Hoby chuckled. "My ma used to say a man should always have somethin' he does that he's proud of."

"Your ma was a wise gal."

"She was the best ever," Hoby said sadly. He took a deep breath and shook himself, and once again his eyes were laughing at the world. "Now then," he said, fixing them on Fargo, "what to do about you?"

"I vote you let me go on breathing."

"Your vote don't count. Only mine does." Hoby sat back. "They must be pretty mad at me in town over robbin' the bank and shootin' big ears."

"They're in shock, mostly," Fargo said.

"Who does the marshal have with him besides that useless deputy of his?"

"Some townsmen and some punchers."

"Hands from the Lazy J?"

Fargo nodded.

"Cowpokes can be reckless. They catch up to us, there might be shootin'."

Fargo thought that was a ridiculous remark. "They're after you to bring you in."

"Or kill me," Hoby said, and chuckled. "You wouldn't believe the low opinion folks in this territory have of me."

"It must be all that robbing and killing."

"It's not like I do it every day," Hoby said. "Sometimes a whole month will go by and I don't rob or kill anybody."

Over at the spring, Amanda Brenner raised a hand as if she were in school. "Can I come over and join you?"

"No," Hoby said.

"Please."

"You promise to behave? Act as you should and not contrary?"

"I promise."

"Then come ahead. But if you don't keep your word, I'll by-God wallop you," Hoby warned her.

"You hit women?" Fargo said.

"Only when they deserve it."

Amanda rose and demurely clasped her hands in front of her, taking small steps. "See? I'm behavin'."

Hoby's mouth curled in a frown. "If there's anything more aggravatin' than females, I've yet to come across it."

"Didn't your mother tell you that insulting a lady is bad manners," Amanda said.

"Don't bring my ma into this. Don't ever bring my ma into anything."

Amanda tucked her knees and eased down and smiled sweetly at Fargo. "I'm sorry they caught you."

"Makes two of us," Fargo said.

"Mr. Cotton, here, was talking to me over by the spring when he caught sight of you."

"Just my luck."

"No, just his," Amanda said. "Mr. Cotton is always lucky that way. Things naturally break right for him."

"Do they ever," Hoby said. "But what's this Mr. Cotton business?"

"I'm being polite and formal," Amanda said, "as a proper lady should be."

"Hell, you ain't no lady. You must be about the same age as me," Hoby said. "You're still a girl."

Amanda's cheeks colored. "Why, Mr. Cotton. Haven't you heard that females age faster than males? And for your information, I'm eighteen. You, I believe, are only fifteen or sixteen. A mere boy."

Semple Cotton laughed and drew a glare from his younger brother. "I didn't mean nothin'," he said.

"We shouldn't ought to have brought her," Timbre Wilson broke in. "She slows us down. And now we'll have everyone in creation after us. Decent folks don't like it when their women are abused."

"What abuse?" Hoby bristled. "I ain't laid a finger on her Highness and you damn well know it."

"Oh, I like that," Amanda said. "You should call me Queen Brenner."

"Will you listen to her?" Hoby said to Fargo. "Tell me I'm right and women are plumb loco."

"They're something," Fargo said.

"You men have cause to talk," Amanda said. "There's not a lick of sense among the whole male gender put together."

"I could just spank you," Hoby said.

Amanda tilted her nose in the air and turned to Fargo. "Can you tell me how my father is doing? This ruffian struck him back in the bank."

"Ruffian, am I?" Hoby said.

"He'll live," Fargo said.

"Thank God," Amanda said. "This clodhopper hit him so hard, I was worried he'd split my father's head open."

"I'm a clodhopper now?" Hoby said.

"You're a great many things."

"It's like listenin' to chickens cluck," Timbre Wilson said.

"Stay out of this," Hoby snapped. "This loco female is playin' games with us. It's what all females do."

"Why, Mr. Cotton," Amanda said. "I'm just a poor frightened girl doing her best to stay alive."

"You're a damned nuisance."

Amanda uttered a tiny snort and said to Fargo, "If you'll excuse me, I'm going back to the spring. It's clear I'm not wanted here or they wouldn't treat me so rudely."

"I've been polite as anything," Hoby said.

Amanda smoothed her dress. "You're a trial on my nerves. I'll go splash water on my face to feel better."

"Don't you dare try," Hoby said.

"I can do as I please, thank you very much, Mr. Cotton," Amanda said, and started to rise.

Lunging, Hoby caught her by the arm. "No means no, consarn you. You can take this ladylike silliness too far."

"You have no couth, sir."

"I don't even know what that is."

"Of course you don't. Now unhand me. Or is it your intention to rape me in front of all these others?"

A look of utter astonishment came over Hoby Cotton. "Where do you get this stuff? I've never raped a gal in my life."

"Says you."

"I kill and I rob but I don't ever violate women."

"Says you," Amanda said again. "You look like a rapist to me. It's those eyes of yours. Every time you look at me, I can tell that you're thinking you'd like to have your way with me."

Semple and Granger and Abe Foreman laughed, and Hoby turned beet red.

"Someone find me a stick," he said.

"You're not taking any switch to me," Amanda said.

Hoby's blue eyes weren't laughing anymore. "I will by-God beat you black and blue."

10

Fargo was dumbfounded. For Amanda Brenner to mention rape was downright careless. It was like tossing a haunch of venison in front of starving wolves. "It might help if everyone calmed down."

"I am perfectly calm, thank you very much," Amanda said.

"I'm calm, too," Hoby said angrily, "and I'll shoot any son of a bitch who says I'm not."

"Manners, please," Amanda said. "Don't swear in front of a lady."

"I can only take so much of this," Timbre Wilson said in disgust, and walked off muttering.

"Are you happy now?" Amanda said to Hoby. "You even upset your friends with your antics."

"*My* antics?" Hoby practically yelled, and pushed to his feet. "I'm the one needs to splash water, you have me so fired up." Bunching his fists, he stormed off.

"Isn't he sweet?" Amanda said.

"You're taking an awful chance, riling him," Fargo told her. The boy was as unpredictable as a rattler.

"I haven't begun to rile," Amanda replied.

Fargo figured she was too young to know better. She didn't realize she was playing with fire. "If you want to see your father again, you'd best rein in that tongue of yours."

"I can be mildly tart at times, I suppose," Amanda said. She looked at Semple. "What do you say? You're his brother. Am I too tart or not tart enough or, like that porridge, am I just right?"

"Don't bring me into it," Semple said. "It's between him and you."

"Same here," Granger said.

"Well, you'd think his own brothers would have his best interests at heart," Amanda said.

"Our interest is in keepin' him alive," Semple said. "The rest is up to him."

"He wouldn't have it any other way," Granger said.

Amanda stared after Hoby, who had marched to the spring and hunkered. "He's so young. It's hard for me to believe that so many people are so scared of him."

"Believe it," Fargo said. He'd met a few natural-born killers in his travels who were just as young or younger. "It's not the age, it's how bloodthirsty they are."

"Our brother ain't bloodthirsty," Semple said.

Granger nodded. "Too much blood makes him queasy."

Rufus Holloway broke his long silence with, "We are some outlaws, ain't we? I might as well be mendin' shoes."

"Hush up, Rufus," Granger said.

"If you gentlemen will excuse me," Amanda Brenner said politely, rising, "I'll go apologize to young Mr. Cotton for angering him."

"You ought to leave it be," Semple said.

"Are you telling me what to do?"

"Not in this life," Semple replied.

Amanda smiled and gave a little curtsy and sashayed toward the spring.

Fargo thought she should stay away from Hoby but he couldn't very well jump up and try to stop her. He was astounded at her grit. Where most women would be in tears, she acted unafraid.

"That gal is trouble," Rufus said.

"I told you to hush," Semple reminded him.

The outlaws all looked at Hoby and Amanda, even Granger, who was supposed to be covering Fargo.

Timbre Wilson was over at the horses, going through a saddlebag.

His Henry and Colt, Fargo saw, had been set on the ground near Abe Foreman. He stared at Hoby and the girl as the outlaws were doing to give the impression that escape was the last thing on his mind, and picked up Hoby's tin cup. The coffee wasn't hot but it would have to do. Gripping the cup by the bottom, Fargo started to raise it to his mouth and suddenly flung it in Granger's face. Granger instinctively recoiled. It bought Fargo the split second he needed to spring to his feet. He kicked Granger in the jaw, punched Semple in the mouth, whirled, and grabbed a burning brand.

Abe and Rufus were riveted in disbelief, which Fargo shattered by thrusting the brand at Abe's face. Abe did as Granger had done and jerked back. Fargo sprang past him, flung the brand at Rufus, and scooped up the Henry and the Colt on the fly.

Over at the horses, Timbre Wilson shouted, "Stop him! He's gettin' away, you lunkheads!"

Fargo streaked for the cottonwoods. A revolver boomed and lead whistled past his ear. Weaving, he was almost to cover when another shot, from over by the spring, brought a spike of pain to his shoulder. He didn't stop. He crashed into the brush and broke into a sprint. It galled him to leave Amanda Brenner behind but he had to get out of there while he could.

Behind him the woods crackled and snapped to the outlaws' hurtling forms.

Shoving the Colt into his holster, Fargo gripped the Henry in both hands and ran faster. They'd likely kill him on sight to keep him from informing the posse where they were.

Another shot cracked and a slug struck a bole with a loud thwack.

To discourage them, Fargo twisted and banged off two swift shots at elusive targets. He didn't hit them but they did drop back a bit.

He reached the end of the trees. Ahead was the hill. Expecting at any instant to take lead in the back, he flew with the sun hot on his face and sweat pouring in buckets.

The Ovaro was where he'd left it.

Snagging the reins, Fargo vaulted into the saddle and got out of there. A last shot cracked but it came nowhere near. Then he was around the hill and out of their sight.

He hated to run. But they would be ready for him if he tried to go back for the girl, and he couldn't do her any good dead.

He checked his shoulder. The slug had only creased him. His arm didn't require stitching. He'd bled a little, was all.

Pretty near an hour went by before he spied dust being raised by the posse. They saw him coming and drew rein, apparently figuring he'd do the same. They were mistaken. He rode up, hollered, "I've found them!" and wheeled around again.

"Hold on!" Marshal Coltraine shouted.

Fargo did no such thing. They'd waste more time with him having to explain. He held to a gallop until he saw that the Ovaro could use a breather and slowed to a walk. Only then did the posse catch up.

"Didn't you hear me back there?" Marshal Coltraine demanded.

"I heard."

"Why didn't you listen?"

"The Brenner girl is alive and unhurt," Fargo told him, "and I'd like to keep her that way."

"How much farther?"

"A couple of miles yet."

Deputy Wilkins came up on the other side. "Her pa will be happy to hear they haven't touched her."

"How close did you get?" the marshal wanted to know.

"Close," Fargo said.

"Do they have the money with them?" This from Wilkins.

"I didn't ask."

Marshal Coltraine said, "That was a damned silly question."

"You never know," Deputy Wilkins said. "Some outlaws bury their loot and come back for it after they've gotten away."

"These wouldn't," Coltraine said.

"Did you see Hoby Cotton?" Deputy Wilkins asked.

"I did."

"You should have shot him. He's the brains of that bunch, from what we hear. With him dead the others might go elsewhere."

"You didn't, did you?" Coltraine said in alarm to Fargo. "Shoot him, I mean?"

"No."

"Thank God. If you'd killed him, his friends might do Amanda in out of spite."

"I hadn't thought of that," Deputy Wilkins said.

"That's your trouble," Coltraine said. "You don't think things through."

"I think good enough to know that if we don't rescue that poor girl," Deputy Wilkins said, "she's as good as dead, anyway."

11

When it came to stealth, the posse were clodhoppers.

Marshal Coltraine had them dismount behind the last hill. He had the cowboys from the Lazy J circle to the right while he and Wilkins and the townsmen circled to the left. Once the stand of trees where the outlaws had camped was surrounded, he would signal and the entire line would close in.

Fargo was with the townsfolk.

An Apache could have heard them coming from a mile away. They were as light-footed as oxen. They scraped their soles instead of placing each foot lightly. Norman tripped and nearly stumbled. The stableman kept spitting tobacco juice.

If it wasn't for the dire urgency of freeing Amanda Brenner, it would be comical.

There was nothing funny about what the outlaws would do once the marshal sprang the ambush. Hoby and his wild bunch would fight their way out with six-shooters blazing, and unlike the posse members, the outlaws had no compunctions about killing.

Fargo girded for a bloodbath. He moved ahead of the others so that he would spot the outlaws before they did and maybe pick off Hoby and Timbre before either got off a shot. With them down, the rest might be easier to take.

Gliding through the cottonwoods, he came to where the spring was visible.

He bit off an oath when he saw that the horses were gone. His concern for the girl climbed, and then he was jolted by surprise.

The fire had burned low. Seated beside it, calmly sipping coffee, was the damsel in distress herself.

Fargo was the first to step into the open. He kept thinking it had to be a trick, that Hoby had put her there to lure the posse in, but no, she was alone and the outlaws truly were gone.

Amanda saw him and smiled and gave a little wave of greeting. "You're back," she said cheerfully.

The rest of the posse came out of cover, looking as confused as Fargo.

Except for Marshal Coltraine. He walked over to the fire, shouldering his rifle. "You're alive, girl," he said with obvious relief.

"I should hope I am," Amanda said. "The notion of dying doesn't appeal to me much."

"Miss Brenner!" Deputy Wilkins exclaimed. "We were worried sick about you." He gazed about the clearing. "We thought for sure those animals would do you harm."

"I thought so too," Amanda said. "Especially that Hoby Cotton. You should have heard how he talked to me."

"If all he did was talk, you were lucky," Marshal Coltraine said.

"You still should have heard him. Just ask Mr. Fargo, there. He was here. He knows how it was."

The marshal and the deputy and the other posse members looked at Fargo and the marshal and the deputy both said, "What?"

"When the outlaws caught him," Amanda went on.

"I don't recollect you mentionin' that," Marshal Coltraine said.

"There wasn't time," Fargo said.

"You got caught?" Deputy Wilkins said. "But they let you go?"

"Oh, no," Amanda said. "He got away. And they were as mad as anything, let me tell you."

"You and me will have a little talk later," Marshal Coltraine said to Fargo, and focused on the girl. "So where did they get to?"

"Oh. They figured that Mr. Fargo would bring you right-quick so they lit a shuck. Timbre Wilson was all for staying and killing you but Hoby said no, your silly posse wasn't worth the bother. That's what he called you. Silly."

Deputy Wilkins shook his rifle in anger. "I'll bother him plenty if I ever get him in my sights."

"He's crafty, that one," Amanda praised her captor. "And bold as anything. Do you know that when I brought up that the marshal wouldn't rest until he'd saved me, Hoby Cotton laughed and said you wouldn't be able to do it without his help."

"Why, the nerve," Deputy Wilkins said.

Marshal Coltraine asked, "How long ago did the outlaws leave?"

"It wasn't more than fifteen minutes after Mr. Fargo got away," Amanda said.

"And they just left you here?" Deputy Wilkins asked.

"You see me, don't you?" Amanda retorted. "Hoby said I had served my purpose and he had no further use for me."

"And he never once laid a hand on you?" This from the marshal.

"As if I would talk about it if he had," Amanda said. "But no, he didn't. He didn't tie me or gag me or nothing."

"I'll be damned," Coltraine said.

It must have dawned on Norman that they weren't going to have to swap lead with the most vicious killers in the territory because he suddenly blurted, "God Almighty. This means it's over! We can go back to town."

"You can," said Rollins, the tall puncher. "We're headin' for the ranch. I've had enough of you townsfolk for a while."

"What did we do?" Norman asked.

"We're stickin' together until we get to Horse Creek," Marshal Coltraine informed them. "For all you know, this could be a trick."

"What could?" Deputy Wilkins said.

Coltraine gestured at the girl. "Leavin' her and ridin' off. We think it's over and split up and head back, and the outlaws pick us off."

"That would be something Hoby Cotton would do," Amanda said. "Like I told you, he's a regular fox when it comes to brains."

"We'll rest a bit and then head back," Coltraine said. "If we push, we can reach town by dark."

Fargo was curious. While the rest relaxed, he went to where the horses had been tied. The tracks led off to the northwest. He followed them to the end of the stand and scoured the plain beyond but saw no sign of the outlaws. Convinced they were gone, he turned to go back and took a step and stopped. "What the hell?"

"Hello to you, too," Amanda Brenner said. She smiled and ran a hand through her hair. "Pretty day, isn't it?"

"Why aren't you with the rest?"

"I told the marshal I needed to answer nature's call but I really wanted to talk to you."

"Me?" Fargo said.

"Hoby Cotton wanted me to give you a message."

"Me?" Fargo said again.

"Hoby said he doesn't hold hard feelings over you getting away. He said you were slick and quick. His very words."

Just when Fargo thought he had heard it all. "I'll sleep better knowing that."

Amanda giggled. "He meant it. And you have to admit, for an outlaw he has a sort of flair."

"He's sort of deadly," Fargo said.

"Well, that too." Amanda looked over her shoulder. "One other thing. Once we're back in town, I'd like very much for you to pay us a visit. We have the big house at the end of Elm Street."

"Why should I do that?"

"Why, so my folks and me can thank you proper. Maybe treat you to a meal. My ma is a good cook and I'm not bad either if I do say so myself."

Fargo thanked her but he had no intention of taking her up on her offer. With her safe, all he wanted was to put Horse Creek behind him.

Little did he know.

12

A sharp-eyed citizen spotted the posse a ways off and word spread rapidly. By the time they rode in, a crowd had gathered. The sight of Amanda Brenner provoked cheers and clapping.

Amanda was on the deputy's mount. The marshal had Deputy Wilkins ride double with Norman, neither of whom seemed to like the idea much.

"Why can't she ride double with me?" Wilkins had protested.

"It wouldn't be proper," Coltraine said.

"But I'd never take liberties," Wilkins assured him. "When it comes to females, I'm plumb harmless."

"You're harmless all around," Coltraine said, "and the answer is still no."

Fargo managed to fall behind the rest of the posse and swung wide of the crowd. He needed a drink or three and then he would be on his way.

Harvey the bartender wasn't happy to see him. "No trouble this time, you hear me?" he warned, and touched his bandaged ear. "The doc had to give me three stitches, damn you."

"That many?" Fargo said.

"I mean it. I should refuse to serve you, you walloping me with that bottle like you did."

"Speaking of which," Fargo said, and snapped his fingers at the long shelf lined with liquor. "Monongahela."

Harvey hesitated, as if inclined to refuse. "No hard feelings about earlier?"

"About you lying to the marshal and me ending up in jail?" Fargo shook his head. He'd changed his mind about walloping him again. "I'd say your ear makes us even."

"More than," Harvey grumped, and selected a bottle. "To show I don't hold a grudge, the bottle is on the house."

"If I hit you on the other ear do I get two?"

"Hardy-har-har," Harvey said.

Fargo took the bottle to a corner table and tiredly sank into a chair. Sunset was an hour off. Plenty of time for him to wash down the dust and put a few miles between him and the town. He'd rather bed down under the stars, anyway. Sleeping with a roof over his head never did seem entirely natural.

Settling back, he chugged and sighed with contentment. "Life doesn't get any better than this," he said to himself.

"That's what you think, handsome. You haven't met me yet."

Fargo looked up.

She was on the plump side with a well-rounded bosom and thick lips that curled in a perpetual pucker. Her eyes were evergreen, her hair a russet shade that hung past her shoulders, curling at the tips. Her dress appeared to have been painted on, and when she bent, her breasts threatened to bust free. "I'm Lucretia. I work here nights."

"Marshal Coltraine allows it?"

"Why wouldn't he?" Lucretia said. "He's male, isn't he?" She grinned and winked. "So long as I don't rile the married ladies into wanting to ride me out on a rail, he lets me be."

Fargo pushed a chair out with his boot. "Have a seat."

"Don't mind if I do." Lucretia deposited herself like a queen settling onto a throne. "I hear you went out with the posse today. The robbery and rescuing that girl are all everyone is talking about."

"There wasn't much to the rescue."

"Don't be modest. There's talk that you were taken prisoner and got away. That makes you a hero to some."

"I got caught because I was careless," Fargo said.

"Even so. Do you have any idea how many people the Cotton Gang has sent into the hereafter? Your guardian angel must have been watching over you."

"My what?"

"You know. Like in the Bible. Angels that watch over us and protect us. Everybody has one."

This was a new one on Fargo. He thought of all the scrapes he'd been in, thought of all the times hostiles or hard cases tried to turn him into worm food. "If I do, mine needs more practice. It doesn't guard me against much."

"Maybe it does and you don't know it."

"The only guardian I need is this," Fargo said, and patted his Colt.

"Well, enough about angels," Lucretia said. Leaning on her elbows, she batted her long eyelashes. "See anything you like?"

"I do have a sudden hankering for watermelons," Fargo said.

Lucretia laughed merrily. "I wonder why that should be." She jiggled hers and said, "Me, I have a craving for buckskin. Are you interested?"

"What was it you said about the marshal?" Fargo quipped. "Now I remember. Something about him being male."

"I'll take that as a yes."

"Now or later?" Fargo asked. He thought maybe she'd have to wait until she got off work.

"Now is fine. I got here early and have a whole hour." She ran a fingernail across her left breast. "Is that enough time or would you rather spend half the night at it?"

"My place or yours?"

"You have a place?" Lucretia said.

"The prairie."

She laughed and shook her head. "Not out in the open, thank you very much. Besides, the prairie has bugs and ticks and snakes. Give me a comfortable bed and privacy."

"Is that bed far?"

"It is not," Lucretia said. "In five minutes you can be sucking on watermelons to your heart's content." She rose and playfully crooked a finger. "Follow me if you are up to it."

"I'll show you up," Fargo said.

Her room was on the second floor of a boardinghouse. The furnishings were simple and the bed sagged in the middle from a lot of use.

Lucretia no sooner closed the door behind them than she fastened herself to Fargo and pressed those luscious lips of hers to his. Hers were incredibly soft. Kissing them was akin to sinking into a cloud of perfume and pleasure.

Fargo cupped a breast and Lucretia groaned. He pinched a nipple and she ground herself against his pole.

"More of that, please," she husked. "I like to build up to it."

So did Fargo. Some men preferred to get it over with and go. Not him. Half the fun was getting there.

Lucretia removed his hat and tossed it onto a small table and ran her fingers through his hair. She kissed his ear and licked his neck and reached behind him to pull him against her.

Fargo returned the favor. He sucked on her tongue. He ran his hands over her breasts. He cupped her bottom and dug his finger-nails in hard enough to elicit a gasp. She began to strip and he helped with a row of tiny buttons at the back. She had nothing on under her dress. Set free, her pendulous breasts hung halfway to her waist. Her hips flared wide above smooth thighs, the junction marked by a triangle thatch.

"Like what you see?"

Fargo grunted.

Lucretia tugged at his shirt and together they got it off.

"Look at all these muscles," Lucretia said.

"There's one between my legs, too."

Chuckling, Lucretia placed her hand on his pole. "Oh my. If it gets any higher, we could put a flag on it."

Now it was Fargo who chuckled. Moving her toward the bed, he eased her onto her back and sat to remove his spurs.

One leg crooked and seductively swaying, Lucretia placed the tip of a painted nail on his shoulder blade and from there ran it down his spine. "I can't wait to have you inside of me."

"Works out nice," Fargo said, "since I can't wait to be in you."

"You make me so hungry I could scream."

"You're thinking of food at a time like this?" Fargo said, know-ing perfectly well what she meant.

"Silly goose," Lucretia teased. "I'm hungry for you. For that redwood of yours."

Fargo dropped his spurs to the floor and unhitched his gun belt and turned. "Then let's get to it."

13

The next quarter hour was a blur of creamy breasts and silky thighs. Lucretia became a frenzied inferno of raw passion. She kissed. She bit. She scratched. She braced her legs over Fargo's shoulders and clamped them onto his neck.

She was so soft, it was like riding a cloud. He gripped her hips and levered on his knees, the velvet sensation of her sheath enough to bring him to the brink in no time.

That's where his self-control paid off.

Lucretia suddenly arched her body and her mouth parted. All that came out was a tiny "Oh" and she erupted in an orgasm so powerful, it was a wonder the both of them didn't fall off the bed.

Fargo's turn came a few moments later. The bed bounced and the ceiling seemed to move up and down. Eventually spent, he coasted to a stop and rolled off of her onto his side and closed his eyes.

"That was a good one," Lucretia said.

Fargo would have loved to doze off but she lightly poked him and said, "I think I have about ten minutes until I have to be at the saloon." He felt her start to slide off the bed and then an intake of breath.

"Here now. Who are you and what are you doing in my room?"

Fargo thought she was playing with him until someone answered her.

"Keep your mouth shut, woman, and don't butt in, and I'll let you go on breathing."

Sitting bolt upright, for a few moments Fargo felt he must be imagining things. But no. It was as real as the revolver pointed at his chest.

Timbre Wilson had slipped inside while they were lost in love-making and now he was leaning against the door, smirking. "Surprised to see me, mister?"

"You know him?" Lucretia said.

Fargo found his voice. "He rides with Hoby Cotton."

"He's an *outlaw*?" Lucretia exclaimed.

"Keep it down, you stupid cow," Timbre said, "or I'll take back my promise to let you live."

"Oh God," Lucretia said.

Fargo glanced at his gun belt and Colt, on the floor by his spurs.

"Go ahead," Timbre taunted. "Try for it. I dare you."

"What are you doing here?" Lucretia anxiously asked. "If you want a tumble you'll have to wait your turn."

"Didn't I just tell you to keep your mouth shut?" Timbre snapped. Straightening, he glared at Fargo. "I don't care what Hoby says. You're too dangerous to let live. I've heard how you can track anything or anyone, anywhere."

"Hoby doesn't want me dead?" Fargo stalled.

"The kid gets strange notions. I don't always agree with them but usually I do like he wants. Not this time. Not with you."

"Here now," Lucretia said. "You can't just kill him."

"If I ever meet a female who listens when I tell her to shut up," Timbre remarked, "I'll shoot myself."

Fargo pressed his hands deeper into the bed. He had to try for the Colt. He was as good as dead if he didn't and probably dead if he did, but he wouldn't sit there and die as meekly as a lamb.

"Yes, sir," Timbre had gone on. "You're a threat, and I learned long ago that the only way to deal with a threat is to end it."

"People will hear the shot," Lucretia said. "The marshal and his deputy will come running."

"By then I'll be out the back and on my horse," Timbre said. "They can breathe my dust and welcome to it."

"You'd shoot an unarmed man?"

"I'll shoot an unarmed anybody, lady," Timbre Wilson said, and extended his six-gun. "And it's time for this scout to die."

Fargo launched himself from the bed. Timbre Wilson's six-shooter boomed and Lucretia screamed. He hit hard on his shoulder, grabbing the Colt as he did, and rolled. A second shot thundered and wood slivers erupted from a floorboard inches from his face. He extended the Colt but the outlaw was already retreating out the door. Fargo fired and hit the jamb and Wilson made it into the hall.

Heaving up, Fargo went after him. He didn't care that he was bare-assed. He burst into the hallway and saw Wilson going down the stairs. He fired again and saw a hole appear in the wall behind Wilson's head.

Lucretia was frantically calling his name.

Fargo reached the top of the stairs and stopped. It could be that Timbre Wilson was waiting at the bottom. But no, when he peered over, he heard boots pound and then the slam of the back door. "Damn," he fumed, and turned.

An elderly lady was gaping at him with her eyes the size of saucers. "My word," she said.

"How do you do, ma'am," Fargo said, moving past her.

"You're awful polite for a naked person."

"Someone just tried to kill me."

"No need to explain," she said, and grinned. "You are a sight for these old eyes, young man."

Fargo snorted and ducked into Lucretia's bedroom. She was in mild shock and kept saying, "I don't believe it. I don't believe it."

He was dressed and his gun belt buckled and was jamming his hat on his head when more boots pounded and there were voices down the hall and then the door shook to several powerful knocks.

"This is the marshal. Open up in there."

Lucretia gasped and pulled the blanket to her neck. "He'll blame me for this and run me out of town."

"Don't worry," Fargo said.

"You don't know him like I do," Lucretia said. "He's the cock of the walk and proud of it, and anyone who causes trouble had better watch out."

"You didn't do anything."

"Tell him that."

Fargo opened the door.

"You," Marshal Coltraine said.

"You got here quick."

The lawman looked past him at Lucretia. "I was a block away and heard shots. The people in the street said they came from in here, and a woman downstairs said she saw a man come running down and go out the back, and that old biddy yonder said this was the room a naked man went into—and here I am."

"I was after Timbre Wilson," Fargo said.

"He came back into town?" Coltraine said, incredulous.

"He busted in on us, Marshal," Lucretia said. "I had nothing to do with it. Honest I didn't."

"He snuck into Horse Creek to kill me," Fargo said.

"The gall of that son of a bitch. You ask me, he's the worst of that bunch. Hoby Cotton included."

"The whole gang rode in as brazen as anything to rob the bank," Lucretia said. "They don't seem to care much that you're the law."

"Did I ask you?" Coltraine snapped.

Lucretia cringed against the headboard and said, "Please don't run me out of town over this."

"What?"

"She's afraid you'll think it was her fault," Fargo said.

"And it wasn't," Lucretia said.

Coltraine motioned. "What do you take me for?" To Fargo he said, "I doubt Wilson has stuck around but how about if you and me look for him, anyhow?"

"Fine by me," Fargo said. "I owe him."

Coltraine swore. "First the robbery and now this. Folks will talk behind my back and say I can't keep the outlaws out. I have to show everyone they can count on me to keep them safe."

"The only way to do that is to wipe out the Cotton Gang."

"If that's what it takes," Coltraine said. "I could use your help.

You're the only one in Horse Creek besides me who's worth a damn. What do you say? Care to lend a hand?"

Fargo had a score to settle. No one tried to kill him and got away with it. Maybe Timbre Wilson had been telling the truth about acting on his own. Maybe not. Either way, he nodded and said, "Count me in."

14

Fargo and Marshal Coltraine searched Horse Creek from end to end and found no trace of Timbre Wilson. Not that Fargo expected to.

Within half an hour, gossip about the attempt on Fargo's life was all over town. Everywhere they went, people pointed and talked in hushed tones.

Coltraine was fit to be tied. "See? It's just like I told you. I could find myself out of a job if I'm not careful."

Fargo had never met a lawman so concerned about what folks thought, and said as much.

"You've never worn tin or you'd understand," Coltraine said. "A lawman slips up and he's liable to find himself in hot water. The town council could fire me over this." He touched his hat brim. "I'd best go see the mayor and let him know I have everything under control. Care to tag along?"

Fargo didn't. His stomach had grumbled, reminding him he hadn't eaten since the day before. As he watched the lawman stalk off, he mused that Luther Coltraine wasn't anything like his reputation. Competent, yes, but he wasn't the man of iron he was reputed to be.

With a shrug, Fargo went in search of a restaurant. He'd no sooner ordered beefsteak with all the trimmings when the bell over the door jangled and in came Amanda Brenner. She looked around and saw him and came straight for his table, nodding at a few diners she knew. "Mind if I join you?"

Fargo indicated an empty chair.

"I saw you come in and thought we should talk." Amanda had on a dress with yellow buttons down the front and a yellow ribbon in her hair. She set her handbag in her lap.

"What do we have to talk about?" Fargo wondered.

"For starters, I wanted to thank you for helping to save me from those terrible outlaws. Who knows what they might have done if you hadn't brought the posse to my rescue."

"They didn't lay a hand on you. You said so yourself."

"No. But it was only a matter of time. I saw how Hoby Cotton was eyeing me."

"Maybe he was smitten," Fargo joked.

Amanda took him seriously. "I'm young yet but it's happened so I wouldn't be surprised."

"Modest, too."

Amanda laughed. "I wasn't bragging, thank you very much. I can't help it I'm pretty. But a girl knows when a fella is interested. He sweats and stammers and can't look her in the eyes."

"Did Hoby Cotton sweat and stammer?"

"Well, no. But he's an outlaw. And awful worldly. Did you know he's from Texas? He told me he was born in the Staked Plain country, wherever that is. And that he's lived in Houston and Galveston and other places, besides. But he doesn't like cities and towns much because of all the people."

"And the law," Fargo said.

"Implying what? He's afraid of tin stars?" Amanda snickered. "Not Hoby. He's got more sand than all the men in Horse Creek put together."

"Sounds to me like you're the one who's smitten."

"Oh, please," Amanda said. "You have to admit, though, that a boy his age robbing banks and stages and all, shows uncommon courage."

"Shows not many brains," Fargo said.

"There's no need to be insulting. To tell the truth, I sort of admire him. He lives as he pleases with no one looking over his shoulder to say he can't do this or that." Amanda seemed to catch herself. "But listen to me. You're right. It does sound like I'm smitten when I'm not. At least, not by him. I prefer older men."

Fargo was hoping to eat in peace so to hurry her along he asked, "Is that what you wanted to talk about? Hoby Cotton?"

"Heavens no," Amanda said. She bent toward him and spoke more quietly. "I wanted to tell you I might know where the gang will be tonight."

"How would you know that?"

"I heard the outlaws talking when they didn't think I was listening. It was something to do with them heading for Denver to celebrate with all that money they stole." Amanda lowered her voice even more. "There's an old homestead about two miles north of here. It belonged to some dirt farmer who was killed by the Sioux. The Cotton Gang is going to hole up there tonight and head for Denver in the morning."

"Why are you telling me?" Fargo said. "You should go to the marshal."

Amanda straightened. "I might run into Deputy Wilkins and I can't stand how he fawns over me."

"He's harmless," Fargo said.

"You wouldn't think that if you were female."

"How old are you again?"

"Old enough," Amanda said. "If you want, go tell the marshal yourself. He'll likely rustle up another posse and you'll have to split the reward. Or didn't you know Hoby Cotton and his brothers are worth five thousand dollars, dead or alive?"

No, Fargo didn't.

"All that money can be yours."

"There are six of them," Fargo reminded her.

"You know how to shoot, don't you?"

"I'll think about it," Fargo lied. It would be a cold day in hell before he did anything so foolish as go up against half a dozen killers alone.

"You do that." Amanda smiled. "Well, I've done my good deed for the day so I'll be off." She rose and nodded and walked out.

Fargo's food came. He was famished, and he put Hoby Cotton from his mind to devote himself to an inch-thick steak sizzling with fat, a baked potato drowning in butter, and peas. He washed it all down with four cups of piping hot coffee.

He was in good spirits when he left the restaurant but it lasted only a couple of steps. Across the street, Marshal Coltraine and Deputy Wilkins were jawing with a pair of citizens. The lawman saw him coming and moved to meet him.

"Still no sign of Timbre Wilson. I'd say he's long gone and you have nothing to worry about."

"Have any plans for tonight?"

"After the past couple of days, I reckoned I'd kick back and take it easy. Why do you ask?"

Fargo told him about Amanda and her claim about the Cotton Gang.

"She told you but not me?" the lawman said in surprise.

"I wondered about that too," Fargo said.

"But you came to me, anyway. Good thinking." Coltraine squinted skyward. The sun had almost set and the gray of twilight was spreading. "We'll wait till dark so no one sees us ride out."

Fargo didn't see why that was important but he didn't bring it up.

"If what she said is true," Coltraine had continued, "we can put an end to the Cotton Gang once and for all."

"How big a posse this time?"

"You and me," Coltraine said.

"Is that smart?"

"You saw what I had to work with before. It would be the same all over again. I'd rather have someone at my side who knows what he's doing. And you do."

"What about Deputy Wilkins?"

"Somebody has to stay and mind the town," Coltraine replied. "No, the two of us are enough."

Fargo hoped to God he was right.

15

Stars sparkled overhead when Fargo climbed on the Ovaro and rode around to the rear of the marshal's office. Coltraine's bay was already tied there, waiting.

The door opened and the lawman emerged. "You're right on time. Good." He was carrying a Spencer, which he shoved into his saddle scabbard.

"It's not too late to round up a few others," Fargo mentioned.

"I didn't take you for skittish."

"You shouldn't take me for stupid, either," Fargo told him.

"I was willin' to risk those cowpokes and a few clerks and

whatnot for Amanda's sake, but not now. Let's drop it." Coltraine's saddle creaked as he swung on. "I'm pleased enough havin' you along. Folks consider me hell on wheels but a man's got to know how much he can and can't do."

"We agree there," Fargo said.

There was no moon. The starlight lent a pale cast to the prairie grass and was barely enough to see by. Now and again a coyote yipped and once a streaking meteor cleaved the heavens.

Marshal Coltraine was grimness personified. "They better be there," he commented at one point. "I want to end this."

So did Fargo. The sooner it was over, the sooner he was shed of Horse Creek and everyone in it.

Half an hour out, the silhouettes of hills appeared.

Fargo took his bearings by the North Star. Apparently, Coltraine didn't need to. The marshal never once glanced at the heavens. "You know where we're headed?"

"Everyone hereabouts knows about the Kemp place. It's been there since the town started."

Presently a small square of light broke the night, and they drew rein.

"That would be it," Marshal Coltraine said.

"We should climb down and go on on foot," Fargo suggested.

Coltraine alighted and shucked his rifle. "I'll swing to the left and you to the right."

"Split up?"

"We'll catch them between us. When you hear me shoot, drop them as fast as you can."

"It's better to stay together," Fargo objected, but the lawman was already moving off.

"Hell," Fargo said. The lawman was being too high-handed to suit him. He told himself that Coltraine had been in situations like this dozens of times and knew how to go about it.

Reluctantly, Fargo slid the Henry from the scabbard, and circled. The small square became a window. Judging by how the light flickered and danced, it was a candle and not a lantern or lamp.

The wind had picked up and was cool on his face. He moved slowly so the high grass didn't rustle against his legs and give him away.

Since everyone called it a farm, Fargo figured there would be a farmhouse and a barn. But there was only one building, a small one, at that. It wasn't until he was close enough to throw a rock and hit it that he realized it wasn't made from logs or frame-built. It was a soddy; squares of sod had been cut from the soil and stacked to construct the walls and laid over rafters for the roof.

No sounds came from within. Nor did Fargo see any mounts. He reckoned the animals must be around back. Edging forward, he discovered that the candle had been placed on the bottom sill of the glassless window.

Fargo stopped cold. No one would put a candle there. Especially not outlaws on the run.

A premonition came over him. Instinctively, he flattened. Over a minute went by and nothing happened and he had about convinced himself that he was giving the outlaws more credit than they were due when someone coughed. But not inside the soddy. From outside it.

Fargo raised the Henry. It must be a lookout. He hoped that Coltraine had heard the cough or the marshal might blunder onto him and all hell would break loose.

The smart thing was for Fargo to let the outlaw give himself away. Instead, out of concern for the lawman, he snaked toward where the cough came from. He tried not to make noise but something scraped, his belt buckle maybe.

"Who's there?"

Fargo turned to stone.

"Abe, is that you?"

Inside the soddy someone said, "What the hell is goin' on out there, Rufus? Who are you talkin' to?"

"I thought I heard somethin'," Rufus said.

Fargo centered the Henry on where he thought Rufus was concealed but he didn't shoot. He needed a target.

"Give yourself away, why don't you?" Abe whispered.

"I hate this," Rufus said. "I don't see why it had to be us. They should be here helpin'."

"You could have spoke up when Hoby laid out his plan. But I don't recollect hearin' a peep."

"Tell Hoby Cotton no?" Rufus Holloway snorted. "That'll be the day. I'm too fond of livin'."

"Then shut the hell up and we'll do as we were told."

A shape rose off the ground. Rufus Holloway was changing position or stretching his legs.

Fargo held his breath to steady the Henry and fixed a bead on the center of the shape. He was supposed to wait for Coltraine to start the fireworks but the marshal was taking too long.

Smiling grimly, Fargo twitched his trigger finger.

16

At the blast there was a sharp cry of pain and then an oath. The night stabbed with flame and answering shots sizzled the air uncomfortably close to Fargo's head. He rolled, levered another cartridge into the Henry's chamber, and fired again.

From the soddy window came a bleat of "What the hell?" The candle was extinguished and a rifle boomed.

Rufus and Abe were shooting wild and lead thwacked the ground all around.

Heaving upright, Fargo ran for the side of the soddy. Rufus must have spotted him because lead clipped a whang on his sleeve. He ducked around and the shooting stopped, and in the sudden silence his ears rang.

Fargo pressed his back to the wall and swore he felt it move. Turning, he discovered that it was partially buckled from age and neglect.

A sound prompted him to peer out. He was sure he'd hit Rufus but he must have missed his vitals.

Another sound, from inside the soddy, let him know that Abe was still in there. He focused on the doorway, the only way out. Or so he thought.

A form abruptly dived through the window.

Fargo snapped a shot, and so did Abe, in midair. The slug thudded into a clod of grass next to Fargo's face, causing him to jerk back. When he looked out again, Abe was melting into the dark.

Fargo wanted to kick himself. He'd had a chance at both and blown it. Now he must go after them.

Tucking at the waist, he darted out. He reached the spot where he thought Rufus had been and stopped and crouched to listen. He figured they might go for their horses and fan the breeze but the night was as still as a cemetery.

They were out there somewhere, intent on finishing him off.

Fargo stalked them. He was wary of shooting at anything that moved; it could be the marshal.

Off in the night there was a scuffing sound.

Fargo stopped. The trick to playing cat and mouse was to move as little as possible. He waited for them to give themselves away, aware that Rufus and Abe were probably doing the same.

Something moved off to his right.

Fargo trained the Henry. Whoever it was, they were coming toward him. A few more steps and he could send them to hell. Then he caught a faint gleam on the figure's chest, the glint of metal reflecting starlight. "Coltraine!" he whispered.

The marshal darted over and hunkered. "Here you are. What the hell happened? You were supposed to wait for me to shoot."

Scanning for sign of the outlaws, Fargo whispered, "You took too long. I had a chance at Rufus and took it."

"Did you drop him?"

"No."

"You should have waited. Now we're up against all six."

"Only two. Rufus and Abe."

"You don't say." Coltraine peered toward the soddy. "They could be anywhere. I'll go check the sodbuster's."

"They're not there."

"It never hurts to be sure."

Before Fargo could object, the lawman dashed off.

Simmering, Fargo stayed put. If Coltraine wanted his head blown off, let him go running around. Fargo would be damned if he'd make the same mistake.

Long minutes of silence followed. The coyotes had gone quiet and the breeze had died.

Fargo could crouch there all night if he had to. He thought about what Rufus and Abe had said and a cold anger festered.

Unexpectedly, Marshal Coltraine came running back. "No sign of them in the soddy. I reckon they're gone."

"You could be wrong."

"Maybe. But I'm no good at twiddling my thumbs. We might as well head for town."

"After you," Fargo said, motioning.

The lawman's reputation for fearlessness was well deserved. Standing, he made for where they had left their horses.

Fargo trailed a few steps behind. He wasn't as willing to gamble his hide on a hunch. But they reached the Ovaro and the bay without being fired at.

Still not satisfied it was safe, he rode with his hand on his Colt.

They had gone about a quarter of a mile when Marshal Coltraine slowed so the Ovaro could come up alongside. "Well, that was a disappointment. I'd hoped to buck them out permanent."

"They knew we were coming."

"How could they?"

"They were lying in wait for us, I tell you."

"You're mistaken," Coltraine insisted. "I didn't tell a soul what we were up to. How about you?"

"No."

"Then they couldn't have."

"You're forgetting who told us the outlaws would be there."

"Amanda Brenner? You're sayin' she's in cahoots with the Cotton Gang?" Coltraine gave a curt laugh. "That's plumb ridiculous."

"I heard Rufus and Abe talking," Fargo enlightened him. "Hoby Cotton sent them to kill us. He wouldn't have unless he knew in advance."

"Listen to yourself," Coltraine said. "After all that poor girl has been through, how can you accuse her?"

"What has she been through?"

"Did one of those shots glance off your noggin? You helped track her down and save her from her ordeal."

"What ordeal?" Fargo said. "Hoby and his gang never laid a finger on her."

"They abducted her at gunpoint. That was enough."

"Are you defending her because she's the banker's daughter? Or because you just refuse to see it?"

"See what? Amanda Brenner is as fine a young lady as I've ever met. She's not one of those gals who puts on airs because she's well to do or likes her own looks. She's down to earth. Sweet. Considerate."

"Marry her, why don't you?"

"I should slug you," Coltraine said.

"Will you at least question her? Make her admit the truth?"

"There's no truth to admit. I won't have you questionin' her, either. She's been through enough. You hear me?"

"I'm right here."

"I mean it. If I hear you've been pesterin' her, I'll take it personal. Leave things like that to me."

Fargo didn't respond. He'd already made up his mind what he was going to do. He didn't like having a bull's-eye painted on his buckskins by a devious little filly. He didn't like it at all.

17

"I'm coming, I'm coming, hold your horses."

Fargo knocked again, lightly so as not to rouse the other boarders. His saddlebags were over his shoulder and his Henry in his other hand.

A ribbon of light appeared under the door. A bolt rasped and the latch turned and Lucretia peered sleepily out. She had on a lacy nightdress and a gown she had hastily thrown over it but forgotten to tie. "You!" she exclaimed.

"Wake everyone up, why don't you?"

Lucretia opened the door wide. "Sorry. I didn't think I'd ever see you again."

"Why not? It wasn't you who tried to kill me." Entering, Fargo set his saddlebags on the small table and his rifle beside them.

"What time is it, anyhow?" Lucretia closed the door and threw the bolt. "I turned in at midnight."

"About two in the morning."

Lucretia's huge breasts were practically spilling from her nightdress, and lower down a triangle showed. "What have you been up to? You didn't stop at the saloon earlier."

"What can you tell me about Amanda Brenner?"

"The girl who was taken?" Lucretia shrugged. "Not much. I see her around and pass her on the street now and then but she never so much as says howdy. But then, the so-called decent ladies hardly ever do. I'm a blight on the female gender—don't you know?" She uttered a sad little laugh.

"You haven't heard anything?" Fargo fished. "Rumors? Gossip?"

"About Amanda Brenner? She's, what, eighteen? And her pa is one of the moneybags in town. That's all I know."

"Does he ever come to the saloon?"

"Her pa? Hell, from what I hear, he doesn't drink. Maybe wine now and then with his meals but he shuns the hard stuff."

"Too bad," Fargo said.

"What's this about? What are you trying to find out?"

"Whether Amanda Brenner is the saint the marshal makes her out to be," Fargo said.

"I can't help you there, handsome," Lucretia said. "Although now that I think about it, I seem to recollect hearing that she has herself a beau. One of the local boys, I'd imagine."

"Where did you hear that?"

Lucretia knit her brow. "Someone at the saloon. But I can't recollect who or even when."

Fargo removed his hat and placed it on his saddlebags and pried at his belt buckle with his thumb.

"Oh my," Lucretia said playfully. "Are you fixing to shed your duds? Should I pretend I'm modest and look away?"

"If you want."

"I don't. That body of yours is mighty easy on the eyes. I can't get enough." As if to prove her point, Lucretia helped him tug out of his buckskin shirt, then molded her fingers to his chest and his abdomen. "I do so love a man with muscles."

Fargo cupped her left breast while running his other hand down her thigh. "Can you guess what I like?"

"Women," Lucretia said.

"Good guess."

She swooped her mouth to his and they enjoyed a lingering kiss that ended when she pulled back and let out a long breath. "Whew. You about curl my toes. I will miss you when you're gone."

"None of that."

"I know, I know." Lucretia kissed his ear and licked his neck and did something no woman had ever done before: she sucked on his collarbone.

"Now I'm a chicken?" Fargo said.

"I could eat you alive," Lucretia said huskily, and ran the tip of her wet tongue from his shoulder to his elbow.

Down low, Fargo was swelling. He grew even harder when she cupped him and lightly squeezed.

"Like that, do you?" Lucretia teased. "You squirm real nice."

Fargo pinched her nipple, and pulled, and she did some squirming of her own. "So do you."

Lucretia nuzzled his neck. "I half think I must be dreaming and you're not really here."

Nipping her on the chin hard enough to make her say "Ow!" Fargo said, "Am I real or not?"

"Real enough," Lucretia said, and laughed. She fused her molten mouth to his and ground herself against him.

A sweep of his arm, and Fargo lifted her off the floor and carried her to the bed. He set her down, removed his spurs and boots, and stretched out beside her. He figured to start right in but she swatted his hand.

"I want you naked first."

"You're awful bossy."

"I'm awful randy."

In no time she had his pants off and dropped them on the floor. She went to press against him and this time he stopped her.

"That works both ways." He gripped her nightdress as if he was about to rip it off.

"Don't you dare!" Lucretia squealed. "This cost me good money." She shed her robe and the nightdress and lay back with an exaggerated sigh. "Now look at what you did. I'm plumb wore out."

Easing on top of her, Fargo gripped her wrists and held her arms above her head. She grinned and parted her legs so he could slide between them.

"Want to get right to it, do you?"

Fargo's response was to rub the tip of his pole along her slit. She shivered and cooed and breathed huskily in his ear.

"Do me. Do me hard."

Not quite yet, Fargo told himself. With a deft dip of his hips, he slid into her but only partway.

Lucretia groaned and her eyelids fluttered. "What are you waiting for?"

A fraction at a time, Fargo filled her velvet sheath. When he was all the way in, he lay perfectly still. Under him, she wriggled and shook and arched her back. He felt her womanhood contract as a powerful shudder ran through her.

"So soon?" Lucretia said in wonderment, and suddenly she exploded in an orgasm that lifted both of them off the bed. She humped fast and furious and opened her mouth wide as if to cry out but didn't.

When, at last, she subsided, Fargo grinned and kissed her. "What was that for?"

Lucretia laughed. "As if you don't know. You sure can plow a trough. Were you a farmer before you became a scout?"

"The only troughs I'm fond of plowing are your kind." To demonstrate, Fargo began to thrust in and out.

"Ohhhh," Lucretia gasped. "If you could do that all night, I'd be in heaven."

"You don't ask for much, do you?" Fargo joked, and settled into the rhythm of his strokes, gradually moving faster and penetrating deeper until he rammed into her as if to break her in half.

Lucretia wrapped her legs tight around him and matched his every stroke. She was an old hand at lovemaking and knew little tricks to incite both of them to a fever pitch.

Not that Fargo needed inciting. His body seemed to burn all over and a keg of black powder was set to go off between his legs. Gritting his teeth, he held off as long as he could. It reached the point where his body refused to be denied, and then there was no holding back.

Afterward, Fargo lay on his side and let himself drift off. He was almost asleep when Lucretia poked him.

"You want I should put the chair against the door? We don't want that outlaw to pay us another visit."

"He won't."

"You sure? The first time was shock enough. And the landlady wasn't any pleased, I can tell you that. I had to beg her not to throw me out. As it was, she went and raised my rent a dollar a month. A whole dollar. And me a working girl who can't hardly make ends meet."

"Lucretia?"

"Yes?"

"Shush."

"I can't help it. I'm all worked up." She kissed his forehead and his cheek and his chin. "You know what would shush me, though?"

"I hit you with a rock?"

"No, silly. We do it again. That should tire me enough that I'll fall right asleep. What do you say?"

Fargo opened his eyes. "Women," he said.

18

The Brenner house was the finest and biggest in Horse Creek. It stood by itself at the end of a quiet street. Maples had been planted and rose bushes grew along a picket fence.

Amanda didn't stir outside until well past ten. She wore a bright new outfit that would cost most women a couple of months' worth of wages, and carried a folded parasol that she happily twirled on her shoulder.

From behind an oak in an empty lot, Fargo watched her stroll to Main Street. Only when she was out of sight did he stride from hiding.

Amanda was on a shopping spree. She spent half an hour in a millinery and almost as long in the general store and was trying Fargo's patience when she went into a small shop on a corner and sat at a table in the window.

Fargo entered just as a pot of tea was being set in front of her by a young woman in an apron. He pretended to be studying a case of cakes and pies and watched her out of the corner of his eye. She filled her cup and was raising it to her lips when she saw him and gave a start. For a moment he thought she would bolt. Turning, he acted surprised to see her and said, "Well, look who it is."

"Mr. Fargo, What a pleasure."

Fargo went over. "Mind if I join you?" He turned a chair and straddled it and shammed an interest in the passersby. "A lot of folks are out and about today."

"It's like this most mornings."

"Do they serve coffee here?" Fargo asked, even though a sign on the wall told him they did.

"Yes. But I only ever have their mint tea. I do so love the taste of mint. Don't you?"

"I'm more fond of whiskey."

Amanda set down her cup and seemed to be pondering what she should say next. Finally she coughed and asked, "Are you going to keep me in suspense?"

"About what?"

"You know very well. About last night. You went to the old farm, didn't you? What happened?"

"The marshal went with me."

Amanda didn't act surprised at the news. "And?"

Fargo looked her in the eyes. "Something tells me you already know."

"How could I? I wasn't there."

"You sent me, knowing some of the outlaws were waiting to kill me. But they were piss-poor assassins."

"That's preposterous."

"I trusted you and I shouldn't have," Fargo said. "But how was I to know you're a conniving little bitch?"

Amanda colored and clenched a fist. "How dare you talk to me that way."

"It's easy. Want me to do it again?"

She glanced around as if to be sure no one was listening. "You're rude. And stupid. Why would I want you to come to harm?"

"You tell me."

"Preposterous," Amanda said again. "You helped save me from the Cotton Gang. I owe you my life, and you accuse me of plotting to take yours?"

"Someone set up the ambush."

"And it had to be me?"

"I sure didn't. And I don't think it was the marshal."

"So I'm some sort of mastermind now? I run the Cotton bunch? I had them rob my father's bank and abduct me? You met Hoby Cotton. Can you imagine anyone telling him what to do? Even his own father couldn't stop that boy from . . ." Amanda caught herself and gripped her cup and held it as if she were considering throwing it in his face. "I want you to leave."

Fargo didn't move.

"So help me, if you don't, I'll cause such a scene, the marshal will arrest you."

"As a threat that's not much." But Fargo stood, and then leaned on the table. "I take it personal when someone tries to kill me."

"I did no such thing."

"And buffalo fly." Fargo smiled and touched his hat brim and strolled out. He could practically feel her eyes burn into his back. He looked in the window and gave a wave, and it was a wonder steam didn't come out of her ears.

Half a block on he stopped in a recessed doorway. Now that he'd stirred the hornet's nest, he'd wait and see what the female hornet did.

He didn't have to wait long.

Five minutes hadn't gone by when Amanda marched out of the shop. Her body rigid with anger, her expression caused others to glance at her as she stormed up the street.

Careful not to be spotted, Fargo trailed along.

Amanda was making for the marshal's office. She was almost to it when she stopped short and seemed to be mulling something over. Abruptly turning, she crossed the street. For the next quarter of an hour she walked aimlessly to and fro, her head bowed in thought.

Fargo could only wonder what she was thinking on so hard.

Eventually she bent her steps to the bank. She was inside a short while, came out, and headed straight for home. As she went in, she looked back, but Fargo was in the oaks in the empty lot and she didn't see him.

Fargo frowned. He'd hoped to provoke her into doing something that would prove she was in cahoots with the outlaws. But she hadn't fallen for his ruse.

So now what? he asked himself. He wasn't about to sit around and wait for something to happen.

There was only one thing to do. It was a long shot. But with the Cottons and their pards out to kill him, he might as well return the favor.

19

In the bright light of day the sodbuster's farm looked even more run down. The soddy was a crumbling ruin. Another year or two and the elements would bring it tumbling down, a pitiful headstone to a dead man's dream.

Fargo approached with caution. He circled the soddy once to be sure no one was there, and circled it a second time looking for tracks. He continued to circle in ever-wider sweeps.

The untrained eye wouldn't find what he did, or know how to read what he found.

Abe Foreman and Rufus Holloway had left their mounts by a low hill a hundred yards or so from the rear of the soddy. Rufus had been limping when they skedaddled, and drops of blood told why.

Not all of Fargo's shots had missed.

The pair had walked their mounts until they were out of ear-shot, then climbed on and ridden hard to the northeast.

"Got you," Fargo said, and tapped his spurs to the Ovaro.

It was early afternoon, the heat of the day at its worst, and he pulled his hat brim lower against the harsh glare of the sun.

The broken hill country gave way to rolling prairie. After a mile the tracks showed where Abe and Rufus had slowed.

The mesquite, the grass, the buzz of insects, lulled Fargo against his will into a state of drowsiness. He shook himself to stay alert and was glad he did.

A gray tendril rose from a string of trees ahead.

A creek, unless Fargo missed his guess, and the outlaws' camp. He looped to come up on them from the west.

The trees flanked a creek. Once in thick cover, Fargo drew rein. Climbing down, he slid the Henry out.

At that time of year most creeks were dry. This one wasn't, but it was so low, a mouse could wade across it. Still, it drew wildlife from all around. Along its course were the tracks of deer and elk and bear and raccoons and more.

The smell of smoke warned Fargo he was close. Soon voices cautioned him to go to ground. Crawling to a clump of wheat grass, he parted the stems.

A coffeepot was on the fire and the two men on either side of it had tin cups in their hands. Rufus and Abe looked glum, the former especially. His bandaged leg might have something to do with it. Their horses dozed over by some alders.

Fargo could pick them off as easy as anything. He was disappointed the rest weren't with them, but it could be Hoby and company would show up later.

The pair sipped and stared into the flames until Rufus stirred and said, "My leg hurts like hell."

"You were shot, you jackass."

"What a thing to say."

"Well, you were. And bein' shot hurts. Quit bein' an infant about it."

"You'd gripe too if you were shot."

"When have you ever heard me gripe?" Abe said. "Or any of the others? You're the gripe of this outfit."

"Like hell."

"You gripe about everything. About the dust. About how hot it is or how cold it is. Or how the coyotes keep you up at night. Or how your coffee isn't hot enough or else it's too hot. Or how sore you are after a day in the saddle. You griped about your share of the bank money. Not to Hoby, of course, since he'd blow your brains out. But when it comes to gripin', you'd win first prize at the county fair."

"I would not," Rufus said sullenly. "You're always pickin' on me and sayin' things that ain't true."

"There you go again."

"Well, my leg *does* hurt, damn you. You get shot, and then see if you're all smiles."

"It didn't hit bone. You bled some but not enough to worry about and we cleaned it good so you won't get infected."

"You never know."

"There you go again. There are days when I wonder why we're pards."

"Why are you bein' so grumpy?"

"Honestly, Rufus," Abe said. He reached for the coffeepot and glanced over and said, "Oh, hell."

Fargo had risen with the Henry leveled.

"What?" Rufus said.

Fargo thumbed back the hammer so they both heard the click. Rufus went to grab for his six-shooter but even he wasn't that stupid.

"So you do have brains," Fargo said.

"How did you find us?" Abe asked.

"The bread crumbs you dropped."

Rufus's jaw muscles were twitching. "What in hell is he talkin' about? We don't have any bread."

"He's pokin' fun," Abe said. "He tracked us, is how he found us."

"What do you want?" Rufus demanded.

"To shoot you again," Fargo said, sidling closer.

"Wasn't once enough?"

"You tried to ambush me, you son of a bitch."

"Here now," Rufus said, hiking his hands in the air. "That was then. You can't shoot a man who ain't armed."

"Sure I can," Fargo said. "But I might not if you tell me when the others are supposed to show up."

"They won't," Abe said.

"Why don't I believe you?"

"We're to meet them east of town at sunset," Abe revealed. "Until then we're on our own."

"That's right," Rufus said, vigorously bobbing his head. "It's just us."

Fargo hoped they were lying. He'd like to spring an ambush of his own on the Cottons and Timbre Wilson. Until then, he needed to trim the fangs of these two. He made them toss their hardware—nice and slow—and then had Abe tie Rufus's wrists and ankles.

Next he made Abe lie belly-down, and bound his legs. He finished by doing the same with Abe's wrists. "Sit up," he commanded.

Reluctantly, both did. From a distance it would appear the pair was just sitting there.

Fargo moved to where the bank dipped to the water. During spring runoff, the level was a lot higher and the flow had worn a kind of shelf where he could sit and see over the top. He set the Henry in front of him and settled down to wait.

"This is a fine how-do-you-do," Rufus grumbled.

"You're wastin' your time, mister," Abe said. "They're not comin'."

Fargo was more interested in something else. "How did the girl know you'd be waiting for me at the sodbuster's?"

"Girl?" Rufus said innocently.

"Amanda Brenner. She's part of this, somehow."

"I'd fight shy of her were I you," Abe said.

Rufus nodded. "There's others as have an interest in her. Hoby Cotton is one of them but not for why you'd expect."

"Hush, damn you," Abe said.

"It's all right," Rufus said. "This scout doesn't know it yet, but he's as good as dead."

20

Fargo tried to get them to talk more about Amanda but they clammed up. Hunkering, he set the Henry's stock on the ground and held it by the barrel. "How long have you been riding with the Cottons?"

"Goin' on five years now," Rufus said. "Back then it was Semple and Granger. Hoby didn't join up until later, and lordy, he was a hellion from the start."

"You're runnin' off at the mouth," Abe Foreman said.

"What harm can it do?"

"You never know," Abe said.

"How many men has that boy killed?" Not that Fargo cared. He wanted to keep them talking.

"Who keeps count?" Abe said.

"Pretty near twenty, I reckon," Rufus said. "He kills folks like most swat flies."

"I'm warnin' you," Abe said.

"What does it matter?" Rufus said, and gave a peculiar twist to his head.

Abe stared at Fargo and nodded and said, "I reckon it doesn't at that. What else would you like to know, mister?"

"Amanda Brenner," Fargo said.

"Exceptin' her."

Fargo suppressed an oath. "Why haven't you made yourselves scarce? Most outlaws, they rob a bank, they quit the territory."

"We would if it weren't for Hoby," Rufus said. "He doesn't want to light a shuck so we can't."

"We don't do nothin' without his say-so," Abe said.

"It's Hoby's way or he feeds you to the worms," Rufus said.

"Yet you ride with him, anyhow."

Rufus shrugged. "It's not as bad as we make it sound. Most of the time he lets us do as we please."

"With little things," Abe said.

"But when he gives an order, we ain't got no say." Rufus grinned. "Like his order to wait here after we were done at the sodbuster's."

"And his order to meet him at sunset east of town," Fargo mentioned.

"About that," Abe said, and chuckled. "We lied."

Rufus nodded. "We're not supposed to meet him anywhere. Fact is, the rest are supposed to meet up with us."

"Why are you admitting it all of a sudden?" Fargo asked.

"Because Timbre Wilson and Semple Cotton are standin' behind you with their pistols pointed at your head."

Fargo half thought they were joshing. Few men could sneak up on him unawares. But when he turned, there they were: Wilson and Semple with their six-shooters cocked, on the other side of the creek. He debated throwing himself to one side and trying to drop them but he was bound to take lead himself. "Damn me for being careless."

Semple Cotton grinned. "They saw us come up and kept you talkin'. Pretty clever, huh?"

Timbre Wilson waded across, grabbed the Henry, and ripped it from Fargo's grasp. "I'll take that." Sneering, he pressed the muzzle of his revolver to Fargo's temple. "I should gun you here and now."

"You heard Hoby," Semple said. "He wants him alive."

Timbre stepped back and his sneer became a scowl. "You have more lives than a damned cat."

With a sinking feeling in his gut, Fargo said to Semple, "Your little brother is here, too?"

"We all are," Semple replied with a jerk of his thumb.

Hoby and Granger Cotton rode out of the trees with Granger leading the two mounts that must belong to Semple and Timbre Wilson—and the Ovaro, as well.

"Look at what we found," Hoby said with his usual devil-may-care smile. He winked at Fargo and said, "Did you miss me?"

Semple laughed and crossed the creek and relieved Fargo of his Colt. "Wouldn't want you gettin' ideas."

Timbre Wilson tossed the Henry a good ten feet. Gripping Fargo's shirt, Timbre pulled him to his feet.

Fargo balled a fist and Wilson jammed his six-shooter against Fargo's ribs. "Go ahead. Try."

"Not yet," Hoby Cotton said. Drawing rein, he lithely swung

down. "Bring him here. I ain't ever talked to a dead man before so this should prove interestin'." He stared pointedly at Abe Foreman and Rufus Holloway, both of whom looked uncomfortable.

Semple took one arm and Wilson the other, and together they hauled Fargo over. Wilson thrust out a foot and Semple shoved, and Fargo wound up on his knees in front of Hoby.

"Let me kill him," Timbre said.

"I just said not yet." Squatting, Hoby grinned and poked Fargo in the chest. Not hard, but playfully. "Funny. You don't look dead. You don't feel dead. Yet you're supposed to be."

"I don't die easy," Fargo said.

Rising, Hoby moved to Rufus Holloway. "That must be true, huh, Rufus?"

"Now Hoby . . ." Rufus began.

"Why is he still breathin'? I told you two to bed him down permanent, but there he is, as big as life."

"We tried," Abe said. "Honest we did. Somehow he got onto us and shot Rufus, so we lit a shuck."

"Somehow?" Hoby said, and glanced at Fargo. "Mind tellin' me how?"

Fargo saw a way to whittle the odds. It depended on how mad he could make Hoby Cotton. "They were talking."

Hoby glared at the pair. "Is that how you bushwhack somebody? By talkin' him to death?"

"We only spoke a couple of times," Abe said. "Quietlike, so no one would hear us."

"The scout did." Hoby turned to Fargo again. "Do you recollect what they were jawin' about?"

"Rufus was upset that Abe and him had been picked to kill me while the rest of you were off taking it easy."

"He was, was he?" Hoby said coldly.

Rufus sat up in alarm. "I never said any such thing, Hoby. Honest to God I didn't."

Fargo tried to remember their exact words. "Rufus said that he hated it. That you should be there helping."

"He's makin' that up," Rufus cried. He had broken out in a sweat and seemed to be tryin' to shrink into his clothes.

Hoby looked at Abe. "Did he or did he not say it?"

"Well . . ." Abe said, and looked apologetically at Rufus. "I can't lie to him, Rufus. Sorry."

"Oh God," Rufus said.

Hoby tapped his chin and scrunched his brow. "What am I to do with you, Rufus? You grouse and you grouse, then you grouse some more."

"Don't kill me," Rufus said.

"You're always complainin'. And now I find you talk about me behind my back."

"Please," Rufus pleaded. "I've stuck with you all this time. That should count for somethin'."

Hoby seemed to consider that. "You know, you're right. I shouldn't up and shoot you. I should let you prove yourself."

"Prove me how?" Rufus asked.

"By doin' what you were supposed to do in the first place and havin' you kill the scout."

Rufus glowered at Fargo. "There's nothin' I'd like more."

21

Holding his wrists up, Rufus said, "Cut me loose, somebody, and I'll do the bastard in."

Hoby turned to Granger, who drew a knife from a sheath on his hip and passed it over. Twirling it, Hoby grinned, and with precise slashes cut the ropes binding Rufus. "There you go."

Rufus held out his hand for the knife. "I'll use that."

"Not so fast." Hoby moved back a couple of steps and thoughtfully tapped his chin with the tip of the blade. "We should be fair about this."

"Fair how?" Rufus said. "Why not just let me kill him?"

"Because I've been a mite bored today." Hoby widened his eyes and made a face as if a great idea had occurred to him. "I know! Let's have a knife fight."

"As in him and me both have knives?" Rufus said.

Semple and Granger laughed. Timbre Wilson continued to glare at Fargo. Abe Foreman appeared relieved that he wasn't Rufus.

"Both of you have blades, yes," Hoby said gleefully. "It wouldn't be a knife fight if only one of you did."

"You can't do this to me," Rufus said.

Hoby cupped a hand to his ear. "What was that? I didn't quite catch it."

"You wouldn't," Rufus amended.

"Somethin' the matter?"

"I've ridden with you all these years and you do this?"

"Rufus, Rufus, Rufus," Hoby said. "You keep bringin' that up as if it counts for somethin'. It doesn't. It's not what you've done in the past. It's what you did to get my dander up."

"I tried to kill him like you wanted."

"Only you gabbed when you shouldn't have. He heard you. And worse, you were complainin' about me."

"I didn't mean nothin' by it. Honest. You know how I gripe all the time. Abe was sayin' earlier that I do too much of it for my own good."

Hoby looked at Abe and laughed. "We think alike, you and me. I'm as tired of it as you are."

"As are we all," Semple said.

Rufus gnawed his lip and regarded them as if he'd never set eyes on them before. "I thought we were pards."

"Will you listen to yourself?" Hoby said. "Nothin' has happened yet and you're blubberin' about it. I said we do this fair and I meant it." He reversed his grip on the knife and extended it, hilt-first, to Rufus. "Take this."

As if he were gripping a rattler, Rufus obeyed.

Hoby turned to Semple. "You still got that foldin' knife you always carry around for pickin' your teeth and cleanin' your nails and such?"

Semple nodded and stuck several fingers in a pocket and produced the small folding knife in question. "This?"

"That." Hoby grinned and pried the blade open with his thumbnail and held it out to Fargo. "This is yours to use."

Fargo took it. The blade was about two and half inches long, whereas the blade on Rufus's knife had to be eight inches or better. "You call this fair?"

"You did hear me say I'm bored?" Hoby chuckled and moved farther back. "Give them room, everybody. Rufus, you cut Abe loose so he can scoot out of there. Semple and Granger, keep your guns on the scout in case he tries to be tricky."

67

Fargo was tempted to reach into his boot for his Arkansas toothpick but he didn't want them to know he had it. Moving back a couple of yards to give himself more room to move, he hefted the folding knife. As weapons went it was pitiful.

As for Rufus, he was smiling like a kid who had been given the greatest gift ever. "Your little knife against this?" he said, and wagged his. "I'll carve you to pieces."

"That's the spirit," Hoby said.

Rufus took a step but stopped when Hoby said, "Ah, ah."

Puzzled, Rufus said, "What now?"

"Not so fast, you eager beaver, you," Hoby said. "You haven't heard the rules yet."

"In a knife fight? There aren't any that I ever heard of."

"Of course not," Hoby said. "I just made them up."

Semple and Granger thought that was hilarious.

Fargo was glad they were having so much fun. They might let down their guard. It was a straw but it was something.

"Do I want to hear these rules?" Rufus asked.

"Probably not," Hoby said. "You see, the problem with most knife fights is that they're over too quick."

"Oh God," Rufus said.

"There you go again," Hoby said, "blubberin'."

Rufus clamped his mouth shut and seemed to regain some of his confidence by staring at Fargo's small knife.

"Now then," Hoby said, "this is how it will be." He paused. "When I say go, you go at it. If I say stop, you stop."

"In the middle of the fight?" Rufus said.

"If you don't, Semple is to shoot you."

Semple said merrily, "Pleased to."

"Those are the rules?" Rufus said.

"Silly man," Hoby said. "That was just the first. The second is that there will be no stabbin' or cuttin' above the waist. You do and Semple will shoot . . ."

"What?" Rufus interrupted. "No goin' for the neck or the heart? What kind of knife fight is this?"

"A damned interestin' one," Hoby said. "I want you to go for his pecker and him to go for yours."

"What?"

"Say that one more time. I dare you."

Rufus opened his mouth, then closed it again.

"Now then," Hoby continued. "The only place you can stab the other fella is in the pecker or the leg. Anywhere else and Semple will shoot you. It's the pecker to win and only the pecker."

"Just the pecker?" Rufus said.

"I swear," Hoby said.

"What?"

A flick of Hoby's hand and his Colt was in it. He pointed it at Rufus's leg but after a couple of seconds he twirled it back into his holster. "No. You're already hurt. It wouldn't be right."

"Why would you shoot me?" Rufus asked.

Hoby looked at Fargo. "I hope you win."

"What?" Rufus said.

"God, I hope you win."

Fargo wagged the folding knife. "With this little thing?"

Hoby showed all his teeth and grandly gestured. "Gentlemen. Are you ready for the world's first-ever pecker duel?"

"I never thought my life would come to this," Rufus said.

"When I say go, you go," Hoby said. He looked at Rufus and then at Fargo and quivered with glee. "Go!"

22

Fargo was crouched and ready when Rufus attacked. Or as ready as he could be with a knife the size of a sliver against one the size of a bowie. He sidestepped Rufus's first rush and skipped out of reach to avoid a slash at his wrist.

"Stop!" Hoby shouted.

Rufus froze in the act of turning. "I almost had him."

"What about 'below the waist' didn't you savvy?" Hoby angrily demanded. "His pecker isn't growin' out of his arm."

"Oh," Rufus said. "I got excited."

Hoby swore, then said, "Semple, the next time he gets excited, shoot him in the knee. Don't wait for me to tell you to. Just do it."

"Sure thing," Semple said.

Hoby gestured apologetically at Fargo. "Sorry about that. You can see how he is at followin' rules."

"There shouldn't be any," Rufus mumbled.

"You try a fella's patience," Hoby said. "Are you two ready to try again?" Raising his arm, he hollered, "Go!"

Rufus came in slower this time, holding his knife a lot lower. "Your pecker is mine, mister," he growled.

Fargo circled, keeping Rufus in front of him and never taking his eyes off that long blade. He jerked back when Rufus stabbed at his groin, and drove the folding knife at Rufus's thigh. Rufus sprang away but not before he was nicked.

"First blood to the scout!" Hoby whooped. "And him with that teeny-weeny knife, too."

Rufus crouched lower and moved his knife back and forth. He wasn't as confident as before. He feinted, shifted, feinted again.

Fargo was keeping an eye on the others without being obvious. Semple and Granger still held their six-shooters on him. Timber Wilson had slid his into his holster but had his hand on it. Abe Foreman hadn't reclaimed his revolver yet.

"Don't take all day at this," Hoby said. "Pretend you are barn-yard roosters and go at it cock-a-doodle-do."

"Cock how?" Rufus said.

"Just fight, you idiot."

Rufus licked his lips and lunged.

Fargo countered with the folding knife but the blade was too small to offer much resistance. Steel met steel and his arm was forced back. Swiveling, he speared the folding knife into Rufus's leg and Rufus howled and bounded out of reach.

Hoby Cotton laughed.

Pressing a hand to the new wound, Rufus cursed and said, "This can't be happenin'."

Fargo rushed him, holding the folding knife down near his knee. Rufus skipped back so fast, he tripped over his own feet and almost fell. Before he could regain his balance, Fargo raked the folding knife across his leg and skipped back.

"The scout does it again," Hoby merrily exclaimed. "Rufus, you are pitiful. Maybe I should find you a sword."

Rufus stared at a fresh trickle of scarlet. Fury smothered his fear, and with an inarticulate snarl, he came at Fargo in a whirl-wind of savagery.

Dodging and weaving, Fargo avoided thrust after thrust. That they were all intended for between his legs helped. He had less area to protect. Rufus struck again and Fargo sliced the folding knife across the back of Rufus's hand.

Retreating, Rufus held up his bleeding knuckles for all to see. "He broke the rules, Hoby! He should be shot."

"No," Hoby said.

"You told us we can only cut below the waist," Rufus said.

"Your hand was below his when he got you," Hoby replied. "That makes it legal."

"You're makin' this up as you go along to favor him," Rufus objected. "I heard you say you want him to win."

"I was funnin'," Hoby said. "If you win I'll be just as happy."

Encouraged, Rufus crouched and became deadly serious. "This time I will do it. Watch and see."

Fargo didn't let himself be distracted by their talk. He focused on that long knife and nothing else. When Rufus charged, he spun, slashed and missed, and they separated.

"Damn it all," Rufus said. "He's too quick."

"Don't give him a breather," Abe Foreman advised. "Keep at him and you're bound to draw blood."

Rufus took the advice to heart. He sprang in, his knife flashing.

Fargo was hard-pressed to spare himself from harm. He blocked, he shifted, he parried. He didn't parry often because the other knife was so much bigger and he was worried Rufus would go for his fingers. For all of half a minute their arms were blurs, and then Rufus retreated once more.

"That was a good one," Hoby said. "Do it again."

"I need to think," Rufus said. "There has to be a way."

"You're stallin'," Hoby said.

For once Rufus wasn't cowed. "I'd like to see you do any better. That knife might be puny but it can still cut."

"The only thing puny here," Timbre Wilson broke his long silence, "is you."

Rufus resented the insult. As if to prove Wilson wrong, he flew at Fargo in a frenzy.

Giving ground, Fargo barely saved himself from a series of sweeps and stabs. Then Rufus made the mistake of overextending, and swift as thought, Fargo stepped in close and buried the pocket knife in Rufus's groin.

Howling in pain and terror, Rufus tottered back. He gaped at the spreading stain and bleated, "Oh God, oh God, oh God."

"Keep fightin'," Hoby commanded.

Rufus had lost his nerve. "No," he said, shaking his head and retreating, "No, no, no, no, no." He backed straight into Timbre Wilson, who shoved him so hard, he stumbled.

"Get back in there, you weak sister."

Tears filling his eyes, Rufus appealed to Hoby. "Please don't make me. I'm hurt. I don't want to do this."

"Did I ask if you did?"

"Damn it, you brat. You can't treat a man this way."

"Brat, did you say?"

Fargo never saw a faster draw than Hoby Cotton's as he cleared leather and shot Rufus Holloway in the face.

Somehow Rufus stayed on his feet and said, "What? What?"

Hoby shot him again.

Semple and Granger were grinning as the body thudded to earth. Timbre Wilson sneered in contempt. Only Abe Foreman showed any regret.

"You have somethin' to say, Abe?" Hoby asked.

"No, sir."

"Good." Hoby replaced the spent cartridges and walked to the body and nudged it. "All this time I thought he was a good man to have backin' me. Goes to show that you never really know someone."

"That you don't, brother," Granger said.

Hoby shrugged. "We'll leave him for the buzzards when we ride out. But first I have to decide what to do about the scout." He regarded Fargo while tapping his temple with the Colt. "The knife fight was a bust. I need somethin' more entertainin'."

"We could always skin him alive," Timbre Wilson suggested.

"Done that," Hoby said. "Too much blood for my tastes. I like to kill but I don't like it messy." He paused. "We need somethin' new. Somethin' we've never done before." He gazed about as if looking for ideas and suddenly snapped his fingers and grinned. "I know. We'll use him as bear bait."

23

The pain in Fargo's shoulders was excruciating. More so than the pain in his legs and hips and that was bad enough.

"What do you think, boys?" Hoby Cotton asked his companions. "Is it a brainstorm or what?"

"He'd draw in a bear sooner if we skinned him," Timbre Wilson said.

"Stop with the skin."

Fargo had been stripped to the waist and his hat tossed aside. They had led him to some trees and proceeded to tie ropes to his wrists and ankles and tie the other ends to low branches, with the result that now he hung belly-down a good five feet off the ground, his limbs spread-eagle, the rope biting into his wrists.

But that wasn't all they'd done. Before they strung him up, Hoby had Semple and Granger smear his chest and back with honey from a jar in their saddlebags.

Hoby had smeared the honey on Fargo in his hair and on his face, then sniffed and grinned. "You smell plumb delicious."

"Brother, you beat all," Semple said.

"Who knows how long it will take a bear to come?" Timbre Wilson said. "And when it does, it might not take a bite out of him."

"Bears love honey better than anything," Hoby said.

"What do we do until one shows?" Timbre said. "Twiddle our thumbs?"

"You're startin' to sound a lot like Rufus," Hoby said, "and you saw how he wound up."

Abe Foreman cleared his throat. "Ain't we supposed to meet"—he stopped and glanced at Fargo—"you-know-who later on?"

"We don't need to leave for hours yet," Hoby said. "We'll have some coffee and see what comes."

Fargo doubted anything would. Not while the outlaws were there. Black bears usually ran the other way when they encountered people. Grizzlies were another story but they weren't that numerous thereabouts. Mountain lions, wolves, and coyotes always fought shy of humans except when they were half-starved. In his opinion, stringing him up was useless but he wasn't about to say so. Not when it bought him a few more hours to live.

The pain grew worse the longer he hung there. Any movement, however slight, flared his shoulders with agony. He held himself as still as he could and tried to shut it out.

Over an hour went by and no bears showed. Flies did, though, buzzing like mad.

The honey also drew wasps and yellow jackets and other bugs. Soon he was crawling with them.

Suddenly a large black wasp alighted on Fargo's cheek inches from his right eye. It didn't seem to like the stickiness of the honey and curled its stinger as if to strike. Wings fluttering, it moved toward his eye. He involuntarily flinched and blinked, and the stinger poised over his eyeball. For a few seconds he thought he'd be stung but the wasp crawled onto his nose and from there onto his forehead.

"That was a close one, huh?" Hoby Cotton said, and laughed.

Fargo hadn't heard him come up. The boy was a ghost when he wanted to be. "Here to gloat?"

"No. I'm here to say I was wrong and ask your forgiveness."

Fargo wasn't sure he'd heard right. "I must have honey in my ears. What is it I'm to forgive you for?"

"This," Hoby said, with a nod at the ropes and the trees. "It was a poor idea. It'd only work if we left you hangin' for two or three days, if then."

"I don't mind," Fargo said.

"Listen to you." Hoby chuckled. "No, I was wrong, and I'm man enough to admit my mistakes. The honey ain't doin' what I'd hoped it would. I need to come up with somethin' else."

"Don't go to any bother on my account."

Hoby slapped his leg and laughed. "You're a hoot."

Since the boy-killer was being so friendly, Fargo sought to take his mind off how to put an end to him by asking, "When are you and Amanda Brenner getting hitched?"

Hoby stiffened in surprise. "Where did that come from?"

"It explains a lot if you and her are sweet on each other," Fargo said.

"For instance?"

"For instance, why she claimed you'd be at the sodbuster's so I'd ride into an ambush. For instance, why no one laid a finger on her when you took her from the bank. For instance, why you lit up like a candle when I said her name." That last was a lie but Fargo used what bait he could.

"Well, now," Hoby said, and chuckled.

"Yes or no?"

"Wouldn't you like to know?" Hoby walked in a circle with his head down and then said a strange thing. "You don't know the half of it. If you did, you'd laugh yourself to death."

"I've never met anyone who laughs as much as you."

"How can I not?" Hoby motioned, encompassing the clearing and the trees and the creek. "It's too ridiculous for words."

"What is?"

"Life. Don't you find it silly, the airs folks put on? Or how they slave their whole life at some miserable job and die old and decrepit? Or how those in high places lord it over everybody else and live high on the hog?"

"How old are you again?"

Hoby laughed, but coldly. "I know. Most my age don't think about stuff like that. It surprises some that I do. I'm a killer and a robber and killers and robbers ain't supposed to use their brain-pan."

"You're something," Fargo said.

Hoby looked at him and after a bit said, "I sure do like you. It's too bad you weren't my pa. Mine never amounted to much."

Here Fargo was, hanging from ropes with honey all over him and talking to the most notorious outlaw in the territory about his relations with his folks. Hoby was right. Life could be plumb ridiculous. "What about your ma?"

"She was as sweet as anything. Could be that's where I get my disposition from. I am nothin' if not sweet."

"You are a puzzlement," Fargo admitted.

Hoby smiled a genuinely warm smile. "It's a shame you have to die. How about you give me your word that if I cut you down, you'll climb on that handsome animal of yours and light a shuck for anywhere but here and never come back again?"

"Can't," Fargo said.

"Why not? I call lettin' you go generous."

"Timbre Wilson, yonder, has tried to kill me. Twice. Abe Foreman and the late Rufus tried at the soddy."

"And you take that personal?"

"Wouldn't you?"

"I suppose," Hoby said. "But not so I'd look a gift horse in the mouth."

"Then there's Marshal Coltraine. He let me out of jail in exchange for my help."

"Ah," Hoby said. "Him. Mr. High-and-Mighty tin star. Did you know that down to Texas everyone adored him? And they adore him here, too. All you ever hear is how good a lawman he is. Part of the pleasure of robbin' that bank was knowin' it would take him down a peg or ten."

"Is it you don't like him or you don't like lawmen in general?"

"The law," Hoby scoffed. "It's just a way to keep folks in line. So we'll kiss the boots of those who put on airs. As for Coltraine, I like embarrassin' him. You could say he's a personal interest of mine." He straightened and sighed. "Enough jabber. I have to decide what to do with you."

"Letting me live would be nice."

Hoby laughed. "It sure would. But since you refuse to fan the breeze, you don't leave a fella much choice." He turned and hollered, "Granger. Get over here and bring that knife of yours."

Granger came at a run.

Fargo tensed. The boy was unpredictable as could be. There was no telling what he'd do. Maybe slit his throat to get it over with.

"Here you go," Granger said.

Hoby accepted the knife and stepped up to Fargo. "I still think my notion is sound but the honey ain't enough. There's somethin' that meat-eaters like more." And with that, he thrust the knife at Fargo's side.

24

Hoby Cotton didn't so much stab as jab. The tip of the knife penetrated an inch or so, no more, enough that blood welled and began to mix with the honey. "There. That should do it."

Fargo had winced at the sting but didn't cry out.

"Blood and honey, both," Hoby said. "If that doesn't bring somethin', nothin' will." He wiped the tip on Fargo's pants and gave the knife back to his brother. "Any last words?"

"Be looking over your shoulder."

Hoby blinked and laughed and clapped Granger on the arm. "Did you hear him? Why can't you be as funny as he is?"

"I'm just me," Granger said.

"See?" Hoby said to Fargo, and laughed harder. With a little wave, he sauntered off.

The outlaws fell into a discussion that ended with the Cottons and Timbre Wilson climbing on their horses. Hoby gave another wave to Fargo, whooped for joy, and rode off with them in his wake.

Fargo was surprised to see that Abe Foreman didn't go too. Abe watched until they were lost in the heat haze of the prairie, then turned and came over with his hand on his six-gun. "You're to finish it?"

"I wish," Abe spat. "I'm not to lay a finger on you. I'm to be your nursemaid, Hoby called it."

Fargo didn't understand. "My what?"

"As punishment for failin' to kill you at the sodbuster's," Abe explained. "I'm to go into the woods and wait for somethin' to come and kill you, then make sure you're dead before I go join them."

Fargo bobbed his head in the direction of Rufus's body. "It could be worse."

"I've had my fill of that boy. Maybe I'll join them and maybe I won't. Maybe I'll sneak off to someplace he'll never find me."

"No, you won't," Fargo said. "You don't have the backbone."

Abe glared, then reached up and gripped Fargo by the hair and savagely twisted his head until Fargo thought his neck would snap. "Don't tempt me, mister, you hear?" He shook Fargo's head and let go. "And one thing you should know. I asked Hoby how long I had to wait around and he said to give it a day. That if nothin' shows by this time tomorrow, I can blow your brains out." He placed his hand on his revolver again. "Could be I won't wait that long. I could kill you now and he'd never know."

"Unless he comes back for some reason," Fargo said.

Abe grew thoughtful. "He just might, at that. He's always doin' what I don't expect." He swore and made a fist. "I'll have to give it more thought." Wheeling, he strode to his mount and the Ovaro and led them into the trees.

Fargo had gained some time, but how long? He tried to twist his wrists back and forth to loosen the rope but all it did was spike new pain up his arms. Tilting his head, he stared at his right boot. If only he could reach his Arkansas toothpick. But it might as well be on the moon.

A dull ache formed in his side. Blood had spread and was dripping to the ground. Not a lot but it wouldn't take much for the wind to carry the scent a considerable distance. As luck would have it, the breeze picked that moment to grow stronger, bending some of the tops of the trees.

Fargo had been in some tights in his life and always gotten out of them. Sometimes through his own efforts and sometimes the hand of Providence played a part.

He was stumped how he could get out of this one. Unless Providence stepped in again, he faced a bullet to the brain.

The time crawled on feet of pain. He kept trying to move his wrists but the rope was too tight. All his twisting did was dig them deeper into his wrists and add to the drops of blood.

It must have been an hour or more after the Cottons and Wilson left that a short bark of a laugh rose from the trees that Abe Foreman had gone into.

Fargo looked over, wondering what the outlaw found so funny.

Then he heard a grunt.

Across the clearing, on the other side of the creek, stood a massive monster with a head as huge as a buffalo's and a razor-rimmed maw that was open as it panted in the heat. The hump on its enormous shoulders, its silver-tipped hair—this was no black bear.

Hoby's ploy had worked. The blood had drawn in not just any meat-eater, but the lord of the prairies and the mountains, the most formidable shredder of flesh and bone on the continent.

A grizzly had come calling.

An icy chill rippled down Fargo's spine as the griz raised its head and loudly sniffed. Turning its head from side to side, it sought the source of the tantalizing smell that brought it.

Fargo held himself perfectly still. Meat-eaters reacted to movement. A fleeing fawn, a bolting buck, would trigger an attack even if a grizzly wasn't on the hunt.

This one padded into the creek. It stopped to dip its muzzle and drank noisily until its thirst was slaked. Water dripping from its nose and jaw, it came to the near side and up over the bank with an agility that belied its bulk.

A fly chose that moment to alight close to Fargo's eye. Instinctively, he blinked and jerked his head. The fly took wing again, and when he looked over at the bear, it was staring fixedly at him.

Fargo had never felt so helpless. All he could do was hang there as the grizzly came closer, ever closer, one ponderous step after another. It breathed in great wheezes that made him think of a blacksmith's bellows.

It stopped not six feet away and sniffed some more, and then came right up to him, to his side where the knife had gone in, and opened its mouth.

Fargo grit his teeth and braced for the bite. He imagined acute pain and his flesh being sheared and his ribs cracked like sticks. Instead, he felt something long and wet slide across his skin.

The grizzly was licking him. It was licking the honey as a dog might lick gravy off a supper bone its owner gave it.

Fargo almost laughed in relief.

It licked and licked, his side, his gut, his chest.

Fargo couldn't look away if he wanted. The bear's musky odor, the puffs of its heavy breaths, the feel of its tongue . . . he should be terrified but he wasn't. It seemed unreal.

At any moment the griz might take it into its head to stop licking and take a bite. Its tongue moved to his shoulder and his neck and then they were nose to nostrils and the bear stopped licking and stared him in the eyes.

Fargo thought his time had come. The bear would get down to business now, to ripping his throat open and satiating its craving for more than honey.

Over the years he had reflected on how he might meet his end. A slug to the head, maybe, or an arrow to the heart, or any one of fifty ways. But he'd never imagined anything like this.

The grizzly sniffed his face and his hair and licked his cheek.

Fargo considered shouting to try to drive it off. The sound of a human voice sometimes did that. But it might also provoke the bear into attacking, and that was the last thing he wanted.

The griz licked him one last time. It grunted, and opened its mouth wide, about to sink its fangs into his head.

This was it.

25

Skye Fargo had been close to death so many times, he'd lost count. He stared into the grizzly's gaping maw as his face was about to be devoured and figured he might as well shout now that he had nothing to lose.

Off in the trees, Abe Foreman laughed.

Almost instantly, the grizzly huffed and pulled back and swung toward the oaks and cottonwoods. It commenced to sniff and turn its head from side to side.

Fargo realized the bear had caught the outlaw's scent. The smell of the horses, probably, too. For the moment he was forgotten as the bear took a few steps toward the vegetation.

Abe Foreman wasn't laughing now.

The grizzly slowly advanced, growling. It was suspicious, and not pleased that its meal had been interrupted.

Fargo wondered what Foreman would do. If he stayed put, the bear was bound to find him. If he fled, the griz might give chase.

Abe Foreman chose the latter. He burst from cover on his sorrel, lashing the reins in a panic, making for the prairie.

For a few heartbeats the grizzly just stood there. Then, with a rapidity that was startling, it erupted into motion and was off after the sorrel in an incredible burst of speed. Over short distances grizzlies were as fast as any horse alive, even faster on occasion, and this was one of them.

Abe Foreman was almost to the prairie when the grizzly over-hauled him. He screamed as a forepaw swiped at his mount's flank. The sorrel screamed, too, a shrill whinny and then another as its rear leg was splintered by a powerful blow.

Abe dived clear as the sorrel pitched forward. His foot became entangled and for an instant it appeared he would go down with his horse but he kicked clear and landed on his shoulder and rolled.

The griz was more interested in the sorrel. It lunged, clamping those iron jaws on its quarry's neck below the ears. The horse kicked and neighed, attempting to rise. Claws raked its side, its throat. Scarlet sprayed in a mist, until, with a wrench of its gargantuan frame, the grizzly bit down and simultaneously broke the sorrel's neck.

Abe Foreman was scrambling on his hands and knees toward the trees. His face was pasty with fear. When he gained the first tree he slid behind it and sat with his back to the bole, quaking from head to toe.

The bear began to eat the sorrel.

Fargo had a reprieve but for how long? Heedless of the torment, he resumed twisting his wrists and pulling against the ropes but all he succeeded in doing was making his wrists bleed worse. He tugged and tugged, his senses swimming from the agony, and wasn't aware he was no longer alone until he heard an oath and was struck a jarring blow to the jaw.

"You son of a bitch. This is all your fault."

His ears ringing from the punch, Fargo shook his head to clear it.

Abe Foreman was red with wrath. Beyond, the sorrel lay with its head attached by a shred to its neck. The grizzly was nowhere to be seen.

"Where did the bear go?" Fargo asked.

"I'm about to splatter your brains," Abe informed him. "That griz is the least of your worries." He gestured. "It wandered off and I am going to get this over with."

Fargo was nearly exhausted from his struggles. He didn't pull away when Abe gripped his chin.

"Rufus is dead because of you. Now my horse is, too. I'm not waitin' any longer. I'm doin' you in here and now."

"Hoby wanted a bear to kill me," was all the protest Fargo could muster.

"The boy ain't here," Abe declared. "It's just you and me and pretty soon it will be just me. I'll take that Ovaro of yours and head for Texas and Hoby Cotton and his brothers can go to hell."

A drop of blood fell onto Foreman's boot and he looked down and grinned. "There's about to be a lot more of that in a bit."

"If my hands were free . . ." Fargo said, but didn't finish the useless threat.

Abe slowly drew his revolver and slowly cocked it and slowly pressed the muzzle to Fargo's temple. "Beg me not to."

"That will be the day."

"Tough hombre," Abe scoffed.

Fargo waited for the inevitable.

"You know," Abe said, and lowered his six-shooter. "On second thought I shouldn't do this quick. I should shoot you to pieces." He aimed at Fargo's leg, then laughed and aimed at Fargo's arm. "Which should it be? Your knee or your elbow?"

Out of the corner of an eye Fargo caught movement in the brush. That something so immense could move so silently never failed to amaze him. "Which would you like to lose?"

"I'm not the one trussed up like a lamb for the slaughter," Abe said.

"You're the one who made the mistake, though."

"And what mistake would that be?" Abe scornfully asked.

"You haven't done much hunting, have you?"

"Some when I was a boy. Get to the damn point."

"My point," Fargo said, "is that if you were a hunter, you'd know that some meat-eaters like to circle their prey and come on it from behind. Wolves will. Coyotes sometimes." He paused. "Bears like that trick a lot. Grizzlies more than blacks."

"That griz is gone and good riddance."

"It probably smelled you," Fargo guessed, "and stopped eating the horse to stalk you. To a griz, one kind of meat is as good as another."

"You think you can think like a bear? You're even more loco than Hoby."

Fargo stared past him. "See for yourself."

Smirking, Abe Foreman turned. The smirk died and terror bloomed and he let out with a, "No! Not me! Go away!"

The grizzly had stalked in the open and was moving toward them with its head lowered and its ears flattened, a sure sign it was about to attack.

"Do you hear me?" Abe cried, and snapped a shot that kicked up dirt in the grizzly's face. "Go away!"

With a tremendous roar, the bear charged.

Abe screamed and spun and ran. He had no chance, none at all. The bear was on him before he took ten steps. Whirling, he fired wildly. Even when the bear bit down on his wrist and he was being hauled to earth, he squeezed off shots.

The rope around Fargo's right wrist suddenly jerked, and the next thing he knew, he was hanging by his legs and his left arm. One of the wild shots had severed the other rope.

Fargo's back was to the bear and the outlaw. A screech raised the short hairs at the nape of his neck. The crunch that followed, and the blubbering, balled his gut into a knot. Girding himself, he looked over his shoulder.

Abe Foreman was on his back, his arms and legs weakly pumping. The griz had a paw on his chest, pinning him, and was almost casually ripping and tearing at his belly.

Abe looked at Fargo and opened his mouth to scream, and died.

Fargo turned away. The horrendous meal seemed to take forever. At last the crunching and chewing stopped and he swore the bear belched. He was hoping it would leave or go to the horse. Instead, he heard it come up behind him. Something wet touched the small of his back and it was all he could do not to recoil from the contact. Warm breath prickled his skin and he felt its tongue.

Not that again, Fargo thought. But the griz licked him only once and walked off. Its breathing and its footfalls faded and there was the splash of water. He looked, and said under his breath, "Thank God."

The brute was leaving. It had crossed the creek and was leisurely melting into the trees.

Fargo let a couple of minutes go by to be sure. Twisting, he bent nearly in half and reached for his boot, and the toothpick. Try as he might, he couldn't quite do it. He settled for prying at the knots on his left wrist with his fingernails. He was at it for so long that he began to think they would never come undone but they did.

Once both arms were free, he clutched at his leg and pulled himself high enough to slid his hand into his boot. The rope around his legs hindered him and he had to jiggle his boot and push but he succeeded in sliding the toothpick out. The rest was easy.

He tried to let himself down slowly but his grip on the rope slipped and he thumped onto his shoulders and collapsed, weary to his marrow. He closed his eyes, tempted to rest. Heavy footfalls changed his mind. He snapped alert and sat up, prepared to battle the griz with nothing but the toothpick if he had to. Only it wasn't the grizzly.

"Hey, big fella," Fargo said happily as the Ovaro nuzzled him.

Using the stallion for support, he got to his feet. The outlaws had shoved the Henry in the saddle scabbard. On a hunch he moved to his saddlebags. In the second was his Colt.

Providence or luck, Fargo didn't care. He was alive. He pictured Hoby Cotton's smiling face and said through clenched teeth, "I'm coming for you, boy."

26

It was night when Fargo reached Horse Creek.

He'd washed his wounds in the creek and had a cup of coffee before heading out but neither helped much. He hurt like hell. His arms and legs were stiff, his side throbbed from being stabbed, and his wrists were welters of pain.

The town lay deceptively quiet under sparkling stars. Voices and laughter came from the saloon but most of the businesses were dark. Most folks were home at that hour, resting with their families.

Fargo drew rein at the marshal's office. The glowing window told him someone was there. He marched in and over to the desk and demanded, "Where's the marshal?"

Deputy Wilkins had his boots propped up and was dozing. He gave a start, jerked up, and blurted, "You!"

"I asked you a question."

"The marshal?" Wilkins said in confusion, and then, "Where have you been? You look terrible."

"The marshal," Fargo said again.

"He's over to the Brenner place. They invited him to supper. Their way of thankin' him for savin' their girl."

"You don't say." Fargo wheeled and strode out.

The Brenner house was lit bright and piano music tinkled on the air. He did them the courtesy of knocking and had the satisfaction of seeing the shock on Amanda's face when she opened the door.

"You!"

"That seems to be popular tonight."

"What does?" Amanda said, and shook her head. "What are you talking about? More to the point, what are you doing here?"

"You're not going to invite me in?"

"After your horrible accusation?" Amanda said. "Over my dead body."

A shadow moved along the hall wall and banker Brenner appeared behind her. "Who is it, Amanda?" Brenner saw Fargo and smiled. "Why, it's the scout. The man who helped the marshal save you." He put his hand on Amanda's shoulder. "Why are you standing there blocking him? Move aside so he can come in."

"He was rude to me, Father," Amanda said harshly.

"Why? What did he say?" Brenner asked.

"I told her I thought she was sweet on Hoby Cotton," Fargo said.

Brenner laughed uproariously. "Oh, that's a good joke, my dear. After what that terrible boy put you through. Now move, I say, and let our guest in."

Her eyes twin daggers, Amanda scowled and gave way.

"I'm obliged, ma'am," Fargo said in mock civility.

"Drop dead."

"Amanda!" Brenner said. "I won't have that kind of talk in my house. Be polite or you can go to your room."

"I think I'll go there anyway," Amanda said, and walked off with her back as stiff as an ironing board.

"You must forgive her," Brenner said. "She has her mother's temper. She can't take a joke for the life of her. Now do come in and join us in the parlor. We were just sitting down to have some brandy. Would you like some?"

"If you don't have whiskey."

Marshal Coltraine was in a chair and rose in surprise. "Where have you been? I was lookin' for you earlier."

"I was picking wildflowers," Fargo said.

Mrs. Brenner rose from the settee and came over and warmly clasped his hand. She was like her husband and on the plump side from too much soft living. She had a nice smile and was one of those women everyone would find likable. "Why, you must be Mr. Fargo, the one I've heard so much about. It's a pleasure to meet you, sir. I'd like to thank you personally for the part you played in saving my pride and joy." She looked past him. "Where is she, by the way? I thought she answered the door."

"She's having another tiff, my dear," Brenner said. "Apparently Mr. Fargo teased her about Hoby Cotton being smitten by her charms so she went off in a huff."

"That girl," Mrs. Brenner said. "You must excuse her, Mr. Fargo. She's sensitive where Hoby Cotton is concerned. I trust you can understand after what she went through."

They offered Fargo a chair. He winced as he sat and was grateful for the glass of Monongahela the banker brought. Downing it at a gulp, he held it out and said, "I'd be obliged for seconds."

"Oh my," the banker said, and laughed. "Rough day, was it?"

"You have no idea."

Mrs. Brenner had reclaimed her seat and smoothed her dress. "We were just discussing the Cotton Gang when you knocked, Mr. Fargo. The marshal, here, is of the opinion they have left these parts and we have nothing to fear from them for a while."

"The marshal is wrong."

"You know that for a fact?" Brenner asked.

"I do," Fargo said, and told them about Rufus and the bear. He spared Mrs. Brenner the gorier details, but when he was done she was still aghast and Brenner was pale.

"My word. The horror you've been through," Mrs. Brenner said. "I don't know if I could have stood it. A grizzly, you say? Why, the mere sight of them gives me the shivers."

Coltraine had been strangely quiet but now he said, "Serves you right for goin' after them alone. You should have asked me to go with you."

"Why, Marshal, that was rather cold," Mrs. Brenner said.

"Everyone knows how vicious the Cotton Gang can be," Coltraine said. "He'd already tangled with them once and should have known better."

"I know better now," Fargo said. "I know I'm going to find out who they're working with here in town."

"What's that you say?" Brenner said.

"Someone has been feeding them information," Fargo said. He didn't say that he thought it was the banker's daughter.

"Why, that's vile, if it's true," Brenner said. "Anyone who would do that should be took out and hung."

"Now, now," Mrs. Brenner scolded. "Don't be perverse."

"There's nothing perverse about justice, my dear," Brenner said.

"And after how they stormed into my bank and killed poor Ed the teller and then struck me and stole all the deposits—" He stopped and then finished bitterly with, "I'm sorry, but every last one of them deserves to die."

"If I arrest them, they have the right to a fair trial like anyone else," Marshal Coltraine said. "It could be they'll get death by hangin' or it could be life behind bars."

"They don't deserve prison," Brenner insisted.

"You're forgetting we must always turn the other cheek," Mrs. Brenner said. "It's not for us to judge."

"There are limits to how much we must stand for. Give people like these Cottons free rein and where would we be?" her husband argued.

"I'm just saying we should be polite about it."

Brenner changed the subject. "What are your plans, Mr. Fargo? I'd imagine you must be eager to quit the town if not the whole territory."

"No," Fargo said.

"You're stickin' around?" Marshal Coltraine said.

"I'm not going anywhere until this is settled."

"How do you mean by settled?" Mrs. Brenner asked.

"Until the Cottons and Timbre Wilson are breathing dirt."

Coltraine frowned. "That's called taking the law into your own hands."

"It sure as hell is," Fargo said.

<hr />

27

Marshal Coltraine glared and Brenner coughed and quickly said, "Enough about that. Let's talk about something else. Why exactly did you stop by, Mr. Fargo?"

"To see the marshal here," Fargo said.

"And to flaunt the law?" Coltraine said.

"To tell you that Hoby Cotton has taken a personal interest in you. His very words."

Coltraine sat up. "What?"

"He said that one of the reasons he robbed the bank was to embarrass you. That teller died to make you a laughingstock."

"My word," Mrs. Brenner said.

"Why does he hate the marshal so much?" the banker wondered.

"Let's ask the marshal," Fargo said.

"How the hell would I know?" Coltraine snapped, and caught himself. "Sorry, ma'am," he said to Mrs. Brenner. "But the scout, here, seems determined to get my dander up tonight. After all I've done for him, too."

"I must have missed that part," Fargo said.

"I let you out of jail, didn't I? I went with you to the sodbuster's. You ask me, I've bent over backward on your account."

"Please, don't spat," Mrs. Brenner said. "I'm sure Mr. Fargo doesn't mean you any ill will. Do you, Mr. Fargo?"

"It's Hoby Cotton I'm after," Fargo said. "And those who ride with him."

"I can't permit that," Coltraine said.

"You can't stop it."

"You're not the law. I am. I won't allow you to run around causin' trouble. In fact, I've just now decided you have until mornin' to leave Horse Creek and never come back. If I catch you here after sunrise, I'll throw you behind bars."

"On what charge?"

"Obstructin' a law officer and anything else I can think of," Coltraine said. He suddenly stood. "I won't be treated with disrespect. Not in my own town. Not in front of friends." He bowed slightly to Mrs. Brenner and nodded at the banker. "If you'll excuse me, I'm afraid I can't stay."

"Marshal, wait," Mrs. Brenner said.

But the lawman was already in the hallway. He didn't look back and in a few seconds they heard the door slam.

Mrs. Brenner wagged a finger at Fargo. "That wasn't nice. You made him terribly mad."

"How very peculiar," the banker said. "If you ask me, the marshal overreacted."

Fargo thought so, too. He stood and touched his hat brim. "I'd best go. Thanks for the drinks."

He half thought that Coltraine might be waiting for him but the yard and the street were empty. He started down the gravel path to the gate in the picket fence and stopped when he heard whispering. It came from around the side of the house.

Gliding over, he peered around.

A second-floor window was open and out of it leaned Amanda Brenner. She was the one whispering to Marshal Luther Coltraine, who stood to one side of a downstairs window so he couldn't be seen from inside.

Fargo couldn't quite hear what she was saying. The lawman responded and he caught the words "Hoby" and "last thing I need." He hoped to hear more and went to edge forward but Amanda whispered something and the marshal nodded and turned toward the front of the house.

Fargo moved to the steps to give the impression he was just leaving.

Coltraine sauntered around the corner, and stopped. "I have half a mind to pistol-whip you."

"You can try," Fargo said.

"I took you for a friend. I was wrong."

"I took you for worth a damn," Fargo said.

Coltraine came over and planted himself. "I meant it about bein' gone by daybreak. Don't make me come after you."

"Do what you have to," Fargo said.

"I won't abide troublemakers," Coltraine said curtly, and stalked off. He went down the street and was soon lost in the darkness.

Fargo stepped to the side of the house and along it until he was under Amanda's window. Groping the ground, he found a few pebbles. The first he threw missed the window and hit the house but the second and third clacked on the glass.

The window opened and Amanda poked her head out. "Did you forget something—?" she began, and stopped in amazement.

"Remember me?" Fargo said.

"What the hell do you want?"

"My, oh my," Fargo taunted her. "Such language from the little lady."

"I'll yell for my parents if you don't go away."

"What were you talking to the marshal about?"

"None of your damn business. And if you claim I was to my folks, I'll deny it." Amanda pulled back and gripped the sash as if to slam it down. "Don't bother me again."

"How's Hoby?"

Amanda hesitated. "You don't know when you're well off. You

should forget about him and leave Horse Creek while you still can."

"I'm not done here."

"What do you hope to prove? What has he ever done to you that you're persecuting him so?"

"Besides stabbing me and hanging me out for a bear to eat?"

"He did what?"

"Anything you want me to say to him when I find him? Give him your undying love maybe?"

"You think you know but you don't."

"No?" Fargo said. "How about if you give him a message for me. Tell him I'm not going anywhere until he's six feet under."

"You're despicable."

"I'll be keeping my eye on you, girl."

Amanda leaned out. "Why me?"

"Sooner or later you'll lead me to Hoby or he'll come see you. When he does . . ." Fargo grinned and pointed a finger and let down his thumb as if shooting a gun.

"It could be you they bury. I hope it is so you'll leave me alone." She drew back and brought the window down so hard, it was a wonder the glass didn't shatter.

Chuckling, Fargo walked out to the street. Down the block a townsman was carrying a bundle into a home. Otherwise, it was deserted. He strolled along, his thumbs hooked in his gun belt. He happened to glance at a dwelling he was passing. Beyond it, on the next side street, a furtive figure in a dress was hastening toward Main.

The figure was too far off to tell much but Fargo was sure it was Amanda Brenner. She must have snuck out the back of her parents' house and was on her way—where?

Fargo turned and cut through the yard. He reached the other street in time to see Amanda go around the corner. He quickened his pace. He mustn't lose her. With any luck she'd lead him to Hoby Cotton and he could end this.

If the boy didn't put an end to him first.

28

Fargo had to hand it to her. Amanda Brenner was good at hugging the shadows and melting into doorways whenever anyone came anywhere near her. She slowed as she came abreast of the saloon and moved with extra caution until she was past it.

Another block and she reached her destination.

The marshal's office? To say Fargo was puzzled was putting it mildly. He saw her peek in the front window, rap on the glass, then turn and dart around to the side and on to the rear.

Fargo had stayed half a block back. Now he closed the gap, paused long enough to be sure the space between the marshal's office and the butcher's was empty, and went down it. A tapping sound warned him to be careful.

Amanda was at the back door to the jail, her arms folded, impatiently tapping her foot on the steps. The door opened, flooding her with light, and she lowered her arms and said, "About time."

Marshal Coltraine had his hat off and a newspaper in his hand. "What are you doing here?"

"I needed to talk to you."

Fargo ducked back as Coltraine started to lean out and look both ways.

"You shouldn't be sneakin' around at this time of night," the lawman said. "What if your folks find you missin'?"

"It's important, damn it," Amanda said.

"Don't use that kind of language," Coltraine said. "You know I don't like it when a lady cusses."

"I'm no lady and you know it."

"Miss Brenner, please."

"Cut it out, Luther. No one is around. Don't be so formal."

Fargo deemed it safe to peek out again. Coltraine was staring at the girl as if he couldn't make up his mind what to do about her.

"You know the rules," the lawman said.

"Your rules, not mine," Amanda said. "Are you going to let me in or not? And if not, you can go to hell and take your badge with you."

"Don't talk like that," Coltraine said. "You know how it is."

"Oh, I know, all right," Amanda said harshly. "Perish forbid that the great Luther Coltraine should turn out to be as ordinary as everyone else."

"Now you're insultin' me. What's so important, anyhow, that it couldn't wait until mornin'?"

"Not two minutes after you left, I heard stones hit my window and looked out thinking it was you but it was that scout."

"Fargo?"

Amanda nodded. "He asked me was I sweet on Hoby and made it plain he's out to do Hoby in."

"Damn him, anyhow." Coltraine took her by the arm. "You'd better come in and we'll hash this over."

"Gladly."

Fargo waited about a minute after the door closed to go over and try the latch. It barely scraped and the hinges didn't creak. He pushed the door open just enough to peer in.

Marshal Coltraine and Amanda Brenner were kissing.

As Fargo watched, Amanda melted into Coltraine and he wrapped his arms around her and cupped her bottom and pulled her hard against him. She let out a tiny moan.

Backing away, Fargo returned to Main Street. He went around to the Ovaro at the hitch rail and coughed and took his time climbing on so that Coltraine would look out and see him leaving town.

He rode east, mulling this latest development.

How could he have been so wrong? he asked himself. He was sure that Amanda and Hoby Cotton were fond of each other. But Amanda and the marshal? Coltraine had to be twice her age. He recollected her saying that she liked older men. And why would a straitlaced lawman like Coltraine risk his job and his reputation by diddling the daughter of the town's leading citizen?

Just when Fargo thought he had it figured out, the situation became more confusing than ever.

One thing he did know. He wasn't slinking off with his tail tucked between his legs. He would see this through, come what may.

To that end, once he was clear of town, he circled and approached from the south. By way of side streets and alleys, he reached the empty lot near the Brenner house without being seen. Climbing down, he led the Ovaro into the stand of oaks and settled down for the night. He was tired and sore and hurting, and he fell asleep almost as soon as he curled on the ground. Some folks found sleeping on the ground hard to do but not him. He'd done it so many times, it seemed more natural than a bed.

He couldn't say how long he had been out when something roused him. A sense of movement. It wasn't enough to wake him entirely and he had almost drifted under again when he was poked in the shoulder and an all-too-familiar voice growled his name.

"Wake up, mister. We have unfinished business."

Fargo opened his eyes. Just out of his reach stood a dark figure holding not one but two revolvers. He stabbed a hand to his holster and found it empty.

"Lookin' for this?" Timbre Wilson said, and wagged Fargo's Colt. "I snatched it while you were sleepin'."

Fargo lay still and tried to collect his wits.

"Hoby sent me in to keep an eye on that damn nuisance of a girl," Timbre said. "Can't tell you how surprised I was to see you come ridin' up." He laughed. "Wishes do come true. I've been hopin' to run into you again."

"Tell me something," Fargo said. "Are Hoby Cotton and the Brenner girl fond of each other?"

"What a stupid thing to ask," Timbre said. "By fond do you mean is he stickin' his tongue down her throat?"

Fargo grunted.

"You're a jackass. You don't know the kid like I do. He wouldn't try to poke her in a million years."

"Why not?"

"I'm not here to talk about him," Timbre said. "I'm here to do what I should have done out on the prairie but Hoby wouldn't let me. What happened to Abe, by the way? When he never showed up, we figured you had somehow gotten free and done him in."

"He's done in, all right," Fargo said. Secretly he was moving his left hand under him to prop his arm for the lunge he was about to make.

"Hoby and his damn games. When someone needs killin' you kill them. You don't tie them to trees and smear them with honey."

Fargo didn't say anything.

"He's always doin' stuff like that. One time he staked a fella out near some red ants and put butter on him so the ants would think the fella was a picnic."

Fargo was calculating. If he moved fast enough, if he threw

93

himself at Wilson's legs and could upend him before Wilson got off a shot, he might turn the tables.

"You're not sayin' much," Timbre said. He trained both revolvers on Fargo's head. "No last words before I put windows in your skull?"

29

Fargo couldn't think of anything to say. He tensed to spring when Wilson unexpectedly glanced toward the street.

"What in hell is she doin' out so late?"

Amanda Brenner was returning from the marshal's. Whistling happily, she swung her handbag from side to side and pranced as if to music.

"Stupid female," Timbre spat. "What he sees in her I'll never know."

"Hoby Cotton?" Fargo said.

"The marshal, you idiot."

Fargo didn't hide his surprise. "You know about that?"

"Why wouldn't I? Hoby's had us keepin' an eye on her ever since he found out about it."

Fargo was more confused than ever. "I don't savvy. What's the Brenner girl to him?"

"You'll never know because in a minute you'll be maggot food," Timbre Wilson replied.

The Ovaro whinnied.

Fargo was as surprised as Wilson. The stallion was usually so quiet, he sometimes forgot it was around.

Out on the street, Amanda Brenner stopped and gazed at the trees. "Who's there?" she demanded.

"Hell," Timbre hissed.

"I heard your horse," Amanda said. "Hoby, is that you? Show yourself. I won't hold it against you."

The Ovaro stomped a hoof and Wilson pointed a pistol at it.

"Damn your animal, anyhow."

Amanda was cautiously approaching. "Is that you, Semple? Or Granger? I've caught you spying on me before. Don't be bashful."

"Stupid female," Timbre said again. He was intent on her, his own pistol still pointed at the Ovaro, Fargo's Colt leveled at Fargo but he had let the barrel dip.

Fargo would never have a better chance. Exploding off the ground, he slammed into Wilson like a battering ram, driving his shoulder into the outlaw's gut even as he clutched at both of Wilson's wrists to prevent him from using the six-shooters.

Timbre Wilson cursed as he was slammed against an oak. He drove a knee at Fargo's groin that Fargo caught on his hip.

"What's going on in there?" Amanda called out.

Struggling fiercely, Fargo and Timbre fell. They landed on their sides and Timbre butted at Fargo's jaw with his forehead. Twisting, Fargo spared himself the brunt of the blow but pain still shot from his chin to his ear. He rammed his forehead into Timbre's mouth and felt wet drops spatter him. Timbre erupted in swearing a mean streak even as he wrenched furiously to break free.

Rolling back and forth, barely aware of their surroundings, they collided with another tree. Fargo's arm was jolted and he almost lost his hold on Timbre's right wrist. Wilson tugged and got loose and raised the Colt to smash it over Fargo's head. Seizing the outlaw's forearm, Fargo drove it against the trunk. Wilson cried out, and then did the last thing Fargo would have expected—he tried to sink his teeth into Fargo's throat.

Fargo rolled, sweeping Timbre with him. They hit another tree. A boot caught him on the shin. He rammed Wilson's elbow to the ground and Wilson's arm must have gone numb because he dropped the Colt.

Timbre Wilson was smaller but he was iron hard with muscle and a dirty fighter. He tried again to plant a knee where it would hurt any man the most. This time it glanced off Fargo's inner thigh but still hurt.

Fargo had to end it. The longer their fight lasted, the more likely he'd be wounded, or worse. Tucking his chin to his chest, he whipped the top of his head into Wilson's jaw.

Timbre Wilson went berserk. Uttering animal growls, he yanked and kicked and tried to butt Fargo again and again.

Fargo was getting nowhere. He belatedly realized they had rolled into the open and thought he glimpsed someone at the periphery of his vision. Bunching his shoulder muscles, he flipped Timbre Wilson under him. Before Wilson could react, he let go of Wilson's forearm and smashed his fist into the killer's jaw. Not once but four times, putting all his strength and weight into each swing.

Timbre Wilson went limp.

Grabbing his Colt, Fargo heaved onto his knees. He had the man dead to rights. But he'd never shot an unconscious enemy in his life. He was debating what to do when a gun muzzle was pressed to his temple.

"I don't think I'll let you kill him," Amanda Brenner said.

Fargo looked at her out of the corner of his eye. She had Wilson's revolver, and it was cocked. "Be careful with that thing. You're liable to shoot me."

"That's the whole idea," Amanda said with a grin. "Lower your six-shooter or I shoot."

"Whose side are you on?" Fargo stalled.

"My own. Now do as I say. I don't have much patience."

"What will your beau say?"

"Who?"

"Luther Coltraine."

"I'm sure I haven't the foggiest notion what you are talking about."

"You and him making love at his office."

Amanda gasped. "You saw us? Why, you lousy peeping Tom, you. I'll shoot you now on that account."

"You'll have a hard time explaining it," Fargo said while slowly moving his free hand toward her leg. In the dark, she didn't notice.

"No, I won't," Amanda countered. "Timbre Wilson will have shot you, not me. Slap him so he'll come around and he can light a shuck after it's done."

"You want me to help you kill me?"

Amanda laughed. "Fitting, don't you think?"

"Fit this," Fargo said. Throwing himself down, he seized her ankle and wrenched her leg out from under her. She squawked and thudded onto her rump and the revolver went flying. Fargo was about to tell her to sit there and not move but she flew at him like a wildcat, raking at his face and eyes with her fingernails. He got his arms up to protect himself.

Fargo clipped her, thinking she would drop like a limp sack of flour. But no. Amanda shook herself and snarled and came at him in a fury. He was trying not to hurt her and doing a poor job of keeping himself from being hurt. Scrambling back to gain some space, he lost his balance and fell. Instantly she pounced, like a cougar on its kill. Wild gleams lit her eyes and her face was a mask of demonic rage. For a slip of a girl, she was ferocious.

Fargo stopped holding back. He punched her in the belly, heard the breath whoosh from her lungs as she doubled over, and followed through with a stroke of his Colt to the side of her head.

Amanda crumpled.

His cheek stinging from where she had scratched him, Fargo got to his feet.

"You little witch," he said. He looked toward the Brenner house and scanned the street to be sure no one was coming to investigate the commotion. Other than the meow of a cat, the night was quiet.

Turning, Fargo figured he would tie up Timbre Wilson.

Only the outlaw wasn't there.

30

Fargo spun right and left, his Colt cocked. Timbre Wilson wasn't anywhere to be seen. Wilson must have regained consciousness while he was battling Amanda. Fargo was puzzled as to why Wilson hadn't helped her. Maybe because Amanda had the outlaw's revolver.

Amanda was out to the world.

Reaching for the saddle horn, Fargo was set to climb on when the front door to the Brenner house opened and out hustled the banker and his wife. They were both in their night robes.

"Amanda?" Mrs. Brenner hollered. "Are you out here?"

Fargo reckoned that they must have discovered she wasn't in her room. He stayed put as the agitated pair bustled to the street and looked up and down it and called their daughter's name.

Amanda stirred and groaned but not loud enough that her parents would hear.

They were talking excitedly. Mrs. Brenner made for the house while the banker hurried down the street, probably to report his missing pride and joy to the marshal.

Fargo's boot was halfway to his stirrup when he sighed and set it down again. Squatting, he slid his hands under Amanda and proceeded to drape her over his saddle. He checked the street before he ventured into the open and spied Mrs. Brenner at the parlor window. She'd see him if he took Amanda over to the house.

He waited, thinking she was bound to stop looking. But no, she continued to stand there, anxiously awaiting her husband and the lawman.

Fargo couldn't stick around. Coltraine would organize a search. The empty lot, so close to the house, would be one of the first places they looked.

Fine, Fargo told himself. There was more than one way to skin a cat, as the saying went. Turning, he led the Ovaro out the far side of the oaks and circled to come up on the Brenner place from the rear. He'd leave Amanda on their doorstep and fan the breeze before the banker and Coltraine got there.

All went well until he reached their back gate. Opening it, he was leading the Ovaro in when a ruckus erupted out in the street. From the voices, Brenner and the marshal and some others had arrived.

Fifty feet more, and Fargo could set Amanda by their door. Carrying her would be faster, but before he could lift her off the Ovaro, a shout from the front yard told him he was out of time.

"You men go up and down the street," Coltraine commanded. "Deputy, look around back."

Spurs jangled, coming closer.

Fargo figured that since the deputy had always been friendly, he'd hand Amanda over and go.

Wilkins came around the corner. He saw Fargo and his hand dropped to his six-gun but he didn't draw. "You?" he said, coming over. "What are you doin' here? The marshal told me he gave you until daybreak to get out of town."

"It's not daybreak yet," Fargo said.

"We're lookin' for—" Deputy Wilkins stopped, his gaze frozen on the Ovaro. "Who's that you've got there? What's goin' on?"

Amanda Brenner groaned.

The deputy looked shocked. "Why is she over your horse like that?" He took a step back. "Good Lord. You're kidnappin' her."

"No," Fargo said. "Hear me out."

"Hear you out, hell," the deputy said. "The marshal was right not to trust you." He resorted to his six-gun.

Fargo slugged him.

Wilson staggered but didn't go down. Instead, he managed to

bawl at the top of his lungs, "Marshal! She's back here! The scout has her!"

Fargo unleashed an uppercut and didn't stay to see the effect. Whirling, he was at the Ovaro in a bound. As he swung up behind Amanda Brenner, angry shouts broke out.

Boots pounded, and someone hollered, "Shoot the son of a bitch!"

Hauling on the reins, Fargo used his spurs.

Coltraine bellowed, "Don't shoot. You might hit the girl. Fetch horses! We'll go after him!"

Just what Fargo needed. He rode at a gallop for over a mile. Any pursuit was left behind.

Fargo mulled over what to do. To the east and south lay hundreds of miles of rolling prairie. To the north, not that far, was the creek where he'd been strung out to be eaten.

He headed north.

Amanda made sounds of coming back to life. She muttered, and fidgeted, and finally her head jerked up and she looked around in confusion. "Where am I? What's going on?"

"We went for a moonlit ride without the moon," Fargo said.

"You! What did you do, abduct me?"

"Not on purpose," Fargo said.

"Let me up," Amanda said, and struggled to rise. "My stomach is so sore, it hurts."

Fargo pulled her up and steadied her while she straddled the Ovaro. Her back was to his chest, and he looped his arm around her waist.

"What do you think you're doing?" Amanda snapped, and slapped his hand. "Don't touch me."

"Would you rather fall off?"

"I've been riding since I was ten," Amanda bragged. "It would take a lot to throw me." But she made no effort to remove his arm.

"Tell me about Luther Coltraine."

"As if it's any of your business."

"He's got to be twice your age or more."

Shifting to give him a look of disdain, Amanda said, "What are you implying? That he's too old for me? Age isn't a factor when two people love each other."

"Is that what it is?"

"Oh my. Sarcasm. For your information, Luther and I have been secretly together for a year now. When he first came to town I thought he was magnificent."

"We're talking about Coltraine?"

"Go to hell. He's tall and good-looking, and everyone admires him so. He deserves better than to wear tin in a two-bit town like Horse Creek."

"Don't let your father hear you say that."

"My pa is a fool," Amanda spat. "He wouldn't approve of Luther and me. Mother, either. They have closed minds when it comes to romance."

"Or maybe just to older men seducing the dress off their daughter."

"Is that what you think? It wasn't like that at all. Fact is, I seduced him, not the other way around."

"You don't say."

"I did, I tell you. Every chance I had to be alone with him, I rubbed against him and touched him to let him know I was interested. At first he didn't pay me any mind. But finally he gave in."

"How long did he hold out?"

Amanda reflected, then said, "Oh, it must have been a whole week."

"That long."

"You're a terrible cynic. Has anyone ever told you that?"

"Read that word in a book, did you?"

"I read a lot, yes," Amanda declared, sitting straighter and thrusting her bosom out. "Which is why I'm so mature for my age. Readers are always more mature than people who don't read. We have more stuff in our head. Knowledge we pick up when we read."

"That explains why I'm so dumb. I mostly only read menus and saloon prices."

"You should try books. They expand the brain. Why, not three years ago, before I started reading in earnest, I was the silliest little thing. All I cared about was what I wore and whether people liked me or not. I wasn't deep like I am now."

"Does Coltraine think you're deep?"

"Oh, yes. He's commented several times on how special I am. He says I'm the most wonderful woman he's ever met. Can you imagine how flattered that makes me feel?"

"And easier to bed," Fargo said.

"You always think the worst. We're like Paris and Helen, I tell you. Or Romeo and Juliet."

"Or horny and randy."

"You're not even a little bit funny. And enough about me. What are your intentions? If you've kidnapped me for lustful purposes, I'll cooperate if you give me your word you won't harm me."

"What?"

"Are you hard of hearing? We should stop soon and get to it so you can have me home by morning."

"What?"

"Why do you keep saying that? Do I have to spell it out for you?" Amanda twisted and smiled and touched his chin. "You can ravish me to your heart's content."

31

Fargo had often heard men say that if they lived to be a hundred, they'd never understand women. In his case it was two hundred. Just when he thought he had a woman figured out, she nearly always proved him wrong.

An old prospector once told him that "Females are the most fickle critters in all creation. They're as contrary and stubborn as my mule. Why the Almighty saw fit to make 'em as a help-meet for Adam, I'll never know. They're not helpers. They're nags. Maybe it's that rib business. The Good Lord should have made Eve from Adam's nose or big toe instead."

"Let me get this straight," Fargo said. "You *want* me to make love to you?"

"That's why you've taken me, isn't it? And yes, so I can get back to Luther that much sooner."

"You won't feel just a little bit guilty?"

"Why should I? You're doing the ravishing, not me. It'll be like in that book I read where the fair damsel was abducted by a dashing highwayman."

"Books again."

"I don't see what you have against them. They're wonderful for the imagination. Why, the first time I set eyes on you, I imagined all sorts of naughty things."

"Yet you say you're in love with Coltraine?"

"What does love have to do with romantic notions? Being ravished is romantic but it's not love."

Fargo had no reply to that.

"So when do we start? The ravishing, I mean?"

"I'll think about it," Fargo said.

"What's to think about? We do it and you take me back. That's what Gentleman Dick Durpin would do."

"Who?"

"That dashing highwayman I just told you about. He was polite as anything and always took the ladies right home."

"You do know that books aren't real life?"

"Please. I'm not stupid. But there's no reason we can't make real life like what we read, is there?"

"I need a drink."

"You're a peculiar man. Here we are, the two of us on the same saddle, as intimate as can be, and all you can think of is liquor?"

"A lot of it would help right about now."

"I'll never understand an attitude like that. Whiskey is no substitute for wanton behavior."

Fargo had to admit she had him there. Fortunately, she lapsed into silence, giving him time to think. He was still thinking when a dark line of vegetation loomed out of the night. Threading into the trees, he soon came to the ribbon of a creek and drew rein. "Hop off."

"Ladies don't hop. They slide with dignity and grace."

"Then slide your dignified ass off."

Amanda harrumphed and put on a show of daintily turning and easing to the ground as if she were setting foot on a velvet carpet. "See?"

Fargo hooked a leg over the saddle horn and sat there with his elbow on his knee and his chin in his hands. "You need to be set straight on a few things."

"Such as?"

"Proper ladies don't bed the town marshal."

"Oh, I'm sure ladies bed people all the time. They're just discreet about it. That's why they're ladies."

Fargo tried a different angle. "What you have isn't true love. Another word for it is sex."

"You're suggesting that all Luther really cares about is my body? Oh, please. He's told me he loves me a hundred times or more."

"He would if he wants sex."

"Will you listen to yourself? Haven't you ever been in love? Really and truly in love with someone?"

"Yes," Fargo admitted. "I have."

"Then you know. I'm in love with Luther. I don't care about our age differences. I'll always love him, and can't wait for him to ask me to marry him."

"When is that going to happen?"

Amanda frowned. "Well, you see, he can't because of my folks. They'd be dead set against it. My father might have him fired. All sorts of awful things would happen." She brightened slightly. "So for the time being we sneak around behind their backs. But I'll be honest. I'm tired of the sneaking." She looked down at the gurgling water and said in a little-girl voice, "I'm hungry and thirsty, too."

Fargo dismounted. He opened a saddlebag and took out a bundle of jerky and offered it to her.

"This is the best you can do?" Amanda said as she took a piece.

"In the morning I'll shoot a buck and serve you venison with all the trimmings."

"You will not. You're poking fun again." She took a bite and chewed with about as much enthusiasm as if she were eating mud. "I never have liked dried and salted meat. It tastes like leather."

"It'll fill your belly." Fargo motioned at the creek. "And that will slake your thirst."

"Drink out of there?"

"It's water."

"But there are all sorts of nauseating things in it. Fish and salamanders and bugs and other stuff."

"It won't make you sick."

"You can't be sure. Fish do their functions in it, for God's sake."

"Functions? Is that a word you picked up with all that reading you do?"

"You know what I mean."

"Fine," Fargo said. "Go thirsty." Hunkering, he dipped a hand in and cupped some water and loudly sipped.

"You're doing that to get my goat," Amanda said.

Fargo dipped and sipped again and let out a contented, "Ahhhh."

"You're mean, too."

"I'll spread out my bedroll and you can get some sleep," Fargo offered, rising. "I'm taking you back in the morning." Or close enough to town that she could walk in while he watched to make sure she got there safely.

"What about the ravishing?"

"There's not going to be any." Fargo stepped to the Ovaro and went to undo one of the ties to his bedroll.

"You don't want to have your way with me?" Amanda asked, sounding disappointed.

"You're in love, remember? It wouldn't be right." Fargo undid the second tie and squatted.

"That's not the real reason, is it?" Amanda said. "Admit it. You don't find me attractive."

"I find you damned silly," Fargo said.

"Well, I never. First you abduct me and now you insult me. Hoby Cotton treated me better than you do and he's an outlaw."

"Did you want him to ravish you too?"

"Don't be ridiculous," Amanda said. "It wouldn't be proper. Hoby Cotton is Luther's son."

32

Fargo could have been floored with a feather. "The hell you say."

"As God is my witness. Why would I make it up? Didn't you wonder why Hoby wouldn't let his gang touch me when they took me from the bank?"

Fargo had wondered but he'd never imagined anything like this. "Back up a bit. If Hoby is Coltraine's son, why don't they have the same last name?"

"Hoby took his ma's name. I don't know all the particulars but she never told Hoby that his real pa wasn't Sam Cotton the whole time he was growing up. It wasn't until a couple of years ago that she finally broke down and did, on her deathbed."

"Son of a bitch," Fargo said.

Amanda had more to impart. "I guess it came as a shock. By the time he was fourteen, Hoby had set his course on the wrong side of the law. He robbed. He killed. And then to hear that his father was the famous Luther Coltraine."

"His brothers are Coltraine's too?"

"Oh, no. Semple's and Granger's pa is Sam Cotton." Amanda lowered her voice as if confiding a great secret. "Their mother was married to Sam when she and Luther, well, you know. That's why she never told Hoby. She was ashamed."

"This was down in Texas?"

"Sure. Luther was born and raised there. It's where he made his reputation. But he decided to leave and come here."

To Fargo it made no sense that a man would leave where he was widely respected for a backwater town in the middle of nowhere. "Why Horse Creek, of all places?"

"When my father and the town council decided they needed a lawman, they put an ad in some newspapers. One was a Texas paper. Luther read it and applied, and who could say no to a great man like him?" Amanda smiled dreamily. "It was fate's way of bringing us together."

To Fargo it still made no sense but he went on to something else. "Did Hoby show up at the same time Coltraine did or later?"

Amanda knit her brow. "About six months or so after, I think. Luther never let on, though, that Hoby was his son. I found out by accident one night when I snuck to the jail to see him and there they were together."

"And the Cotton Gang has been terrorizing the territory ever since."

"What's your point?" Amanda asked. "Luther can't control Hoby any more than my parents can control me. He told me that he wishes Hoby would go back to Texas or anywhere but here but Hoby won't."

"He's doing it to spite his pa?"

"You'd have to ask him," Amanda said. "I did, but Hoby refused to say. I told him flat out he was being unfair to Luther by causing so much trouble and Hoby laughed and said he was doing what was best for everyone."

"What did he mean?"

"How would I know? You saw how Hoby is. Everything is a game to him. He does as he pleases and hang the consequences." Amanda stifled a yawn. "Goodness, I'm tired. I really should turn in."

Fargo finished spreading the blankets and stepped back. "They're all yours."

In the distance a coyote yipped and Amanda gazed fearfully into the dark. "I never have liked the wilds. Especially at night. Who knows what's out there waiting to pounce."

"I'll keep watch," Fargo said.

"Keep a good one." Amanda lowered onto her side with her hand for a pillow and closed her eyes. "This has been a week I'll never forget. First Hoby spirits me away and now you. Luther must be worried sick. He'll scour the countryside until he finds me."

"Get some rest."

Amanda nodded, and not two minutes later her deep, regular breathing told him she had succumbed to her fatigue.

Fargo wished that he could. Shucking the Henry, he moved closer to the trees, and sat.

The night was peaceful. No roars or screams shattered the serenity. It made staying awake that much harder.

Fargo tried his best. When his eyelids grew leaden he tossed his head and swung his arms and once he got up and went to the creek and splashed water on his face. It helped for a while but eventually all that he had been through the past couple of days caught up to him. He dozed off, sitting up.

The piercing squawk of a jay woke him when the eastern sky was just starting to brighten with the promise of the new day. He sat up and shook himself and tried to spur his sluggish mind into working.

"Have a good sleep?"

Fargo looked up, and froze. For once again his sharp senses had failed him. Concealing his surprise, he said, "Morning."

Hoby Cotton's boy-man face split in a huge grin. He was sitting cross-legged, flanked on either side by Semple and Granger with their six-shooters drawn and cocked.

Behind them stood Timbre Wilson. He had acquired another revolver somewhere, and his hand was on it. "Say the word and I'll gun him."

"Don't start with that again," Hoby said. "You'll kill him when I say you can and not before." He made a teepee of his fingers and bestowed another smile on Fargo. "You must be wonderin' how we found you."

"Lucky hunch?"

"I do have more than my share. But no, Timbre followed you out of town. He stayed well back so you wouldn't spot him, and then came to fetch me when you and her settled down for the night."

"Tricky cuss," Fargo said to Timbre.

"Wasn't much to it," Wilson replied. "I stopped and listened a lot. Almost lost you when you turned north."

"Hoby," Semple said. "His guns."

"I'm gettin' to that," Hoby said, and flicked a finger at the Henry and the Colt. "Shed yourself of them if you don't mind and even if you do."

Fargo was mad at himself. This made twice they'd gotten the drop on him. He slid the Henry to one side and eased the Colt out and set it down beside the rifle. "What's in store for me this time? More bear bait?"

Hoby chuckled. "I learn from my mistakes. This time will be different." He flicked the same finger at Granger. "There. His claws have been pulled. Happy now, Semple?"

"You take too many chances," Semple said.

"I like livin' dangerous," Hoby replied. To Fargo he said, "We're not alike, my brothers and me."

"Must come from having different fathers."

Hoby lost his smile and glared at the sleeping form of Amanda Brenner. "Someone has been flappin' her mouth when she shouldn't, sounds like."

"So I know. So what?" Fargo said.

"So you shouldn't." Hoby got up and walked around him and over to Amanda. None too gently he poked her with his toe. She moved her arm but otherwise didn't rouse. "I could be a redskin about to lift her hair and she'd just lie there. If females aren't plumb worthless I don't know what is." He hiked his leg as if to stomp on her head.

"I hear you were close to your ma," Fargo said quickly.

Hoby slowly lowered his boot. "Is that what she told you? The stupid cow. My ma and me were never that close."

"You must have been a hellion."

"Weren't that," Hoby said. "I was a reminder of somethin' she'd done, and she hated me for it."

"That when she slept with Luther Coltraine she was married to Sam Cotton?" Fargo said.

Hoby darkened with barely contained fury. "The little bitch told you that, too?" He paused. "She just ruined any hope you had that I might change my mind about killin' you. Make no mistake. This is your last day on God's green earth."

33

It was then that the sound of the voices finally brought Amanda around. Blinking and rubbing herself, she sat up and looked about her in confusion. "What's going on?"

"This," Hoby said, and whirling, he slapped her across the face.

The blow knocked Amanda down and jolted her awake. "Hoby!" she cried. "Why'd you do that? I thought we were friends."

"You thought wrong," Hoby growled, and raised his hand to strike her again.

"Before you get into it," Semple said, "we should tie them."

"Fine," Hoby snapped. "But only him."

"Why not her?"

"Because I said so."

Once again Fargo had to submit to having his wrists bound. This time they didn't bother with his legs. As Granger stepped back, Fargo tried to divert Hoby from Amanda Brenner by saying, "I'm curious. Why did you come all this way from Texas? To follow Coltraine?"

"He *is* my pa," Hoby said.

"Who didn't have much to do with you when you were a boy, from what I hear."

"He didn't know my ma got pregnant," Hoby said. "She never sent him word she'd had a kid. The first he heard of it was when I showed up on his doorstep."

Semple broke in with, "You should have left it be, Hoby. So what if Ma had an affair? So what if Coltraine was your real pa?"

A troubled expression came over the boy-man. "I had to meet him. I had to find out what he was like."

"What did it matter?" Semple asked.

"It mattered to me," Hoby said. "How was it he was so straight arrow and I was ridin' the owlhoot trail? It seemed to me we were nothin' alike yet he was supposed to have sired me."

"I would have left it be, is all," Semple insisted.

Hoby looked at Fargo. "You can see how it was, can't you? It ate at me, not knowin'. Sam Cotton wasn't much. A clerk and a nobody. But Luther Coltraine. Everybody in Texas knew about him. One of the best lawmen alive. Everyone said so. And I was the fruit of his loins."

Amanda chose that moment to say, "He was glad you looked him up. He's told me so."

"What do you know?" Hoby replied.

"I know I love him. I know that one day I'll be his wife."

"Oh, will you?" Hoby said. "And what, be my new ma, to boot?" He laughed uproariously yet with an edge. "You are so stupid, it's pitiful."

"Why are you being so mean to me?"

"Because you're a cow. Because he's doin' it again and you're so dumb you don't see it."

"Who's doing what?"

Hoby took a half step toward her and balled a fist. "Who are we talkin' about, girl? The great Luther Coltraine. The tin star who can do no wrong. Who all the folks look up to because he's so good and pure." Hoby gazed to the south as if he could see all the way to Texas. "But they don't know the real him. The womanizin' bastard who trifles with females right and left. Who diddled my ma. Who's poked more fillies than you can count. To him you're nothin' but a notch on his pecker."

"You're pulling that out of your hat," Amanda said, shocked.

"What for? To hurt your feelin's? I don't give a damn about you. The only reason I took you from the bank was to get to know you. To find out what you were like, and how he got up your skirts. He did it the same as he always does. He impresses females with how famous he is, then beds them."

"His love for me is special," Amanda said. "He's said so plenty of times."

"And you believe him."

Amanda appeared close to tears. "It can't be true. It just can't. Maybe your ma lied. Maybe she never really slept with him but told you she did so you might change your ways."

"She was dyin' of consumption," Hoby said. "She was close to meetin' her Maker and said she wanted to come clean with me. Don't you dare insult her again or I'll shoot you where you sit."

"Speakin' of which," Timbre Wilson said. "How much more jabber will there be before we get to it?"

"Shut your piehole," Hoby said. "This is important to me."

109

A wave of insight washed over Fargo. Here was this boy who'd strayed off the straight and narrow, who'd become a killer by fifteen, who'd learned that his natural father was one of the most upstanding men alive, who went to meet the paragon and found out that Luther Coltraine wasn't the monument to virtue everyone praised him for being. Who discovered that the one man he thought might be someone he could look up to, was, in fact, as human as everybody else. No wonder the boy was so bitter.

Hoby drew his Colt and pointed it at Amanda.

Recoiling, she thrust out a hand. "What are you doing?"

"Savin' you from him," Hoby said. "Sparin' you the misery he gave my ma all those years."

"But I don't need saving," Amanda exclaimed. "I like being with him and he likes being with me."

"Oh? Does he do it out in the open where everyone can see? Or does he have you skulkin' around in the dead of night so he can make love to you?"

"Please," Amanda said. "Lower the gun. I don't want to die."

"I'm doin' you a favor."

"And Coltraine, too," Fargo said.

Hoby glanced over. "How is it any favor to him?"

"No one will ever know," Fargo said. "You'll have killed the only proof you have that he's no account."

"There's other proof," Hoby said, but he let the Colt fall to his side and stared hard at Amanda Brenner. "The scout has a point, though. If folks found out about you, they'd be more likely to believe the rest of it."

"I'm not about to tell anyone," Amanda said.

"You will if you want to go on breathin'. Or, better yet"—Hoby leveled his Colt at Fargo—"if you want him to."

34

"Go ahead. Pull the trigger," Amanda Brenner said. "How could you imagine he means anything to me?"

"I would have hurt you by now but for him buttin' in," Hoby told her. "He's been lookin' out for you, and just like with Coltraine, you're too stupid to see it."

"Quit insulting me."

"I'll by-God do more than that," Hoby said, once more fixing the Colt on her. "Say your prayers."

From out of the vegetation that surrounded them, which was brightening with the glow of the rising sun, came a bellow.

"You there! This is the law! We have you surrounded. Throw down your guns and raise your hands in the air or we will open fire."

"It's Coltraine!" Granger exclaimed in alarm, and swung toward the cottonwoods and banged off a shot.

"No!" Amanda Brenner cried, but the harm had been done.

Bedlam erupted. The outlaws bolted for their horses while firing in all directions at enemies they couldn't see. Fargo threw himself at Amanda just as a return volley thundered, lead and smoke pouring from everywhere. He slammed into Amanda with his shoulder and drove her to the ground as above them slugs whistled and buzzed.

"Stay down," he hollered in her ear, and rolled off.

The outlaws had targets now. They were shooting at muzzle flashes and vague figures. For its part, the posse was trying to bring the weaving, twisting bad men down, and doing a terrible job of it even though the Cotton Gang was in the open and the posse wasn't.

Plunging his fingers into his boot, Fargo palmed the Arkansas toothpick. It made short shrift of the rope. His Colt and his Henry still lay close by, and sliding the toothpick into its ankle sheath, he lunged and scooped them up.

Lead clipped the earth next to him as he flung himself at the low bank. Whether from an outlaw or a posse member, he couldn't say. Rolling over the edge, he landed in a crouch. He shoved the rifle into his shoulder, worked the Henry's lever, and popped his head up.

Granger Cotton was down. He'd taken a round in the chest. Semple had an arm under him and was helping him up while Hoby and Timbre Wilson covered them.

No sooner would a posse member fire or show himself than Hoby or Timbre would spin and shoot.

From out of the brush a death rattle sounded.

"Aim, damn you! Aim!" Luther Coltraine roared. "Make sure of your shots."

The outlaws were almost to their mounts.

Fargo raised up and instantly Timbre Wilson fanned a slug that kicked dirt in his face and drove him down.

"Don't let them get away!" the marshal bellowed.

Fargo raised his head again. This time it was a clerk who appeared from behind a tree and snapped a shot at him. Fargo was about to yell that he was on their side, and then he remembered. They thought he'd abducted Amanda.

Amanda. Fargo glanced at her and swore.

She had been hit. She was on her back with a hand to her shoulder, grimacing in pain. Blood seeped between her fingers and was staining her dress.

Even as Fargo looked, another slug struck the ground inches from her head. A stray shot, of which there were many. The posse was made up of townsmen who rarely, if ever, used a firearm. They might be able to hit the broad side of a barn but only if they were standing next to it. In their wild shooting, it was a wonder they didn't hit their own men.

Scrambling over the bank, Fargo crawled to her and got an arm around her waist. She didn't resist as he dragged her toward the bank. All she did was groan and say through clenched teeth, "It hurts."

Clamping her to his chest, Fargo slid over and set her beside him. "Let me see how bad it is."

Amanda moved her hand.

The slug had penetrated under her collarbone and exited out her back, leaving a hole the size of a walnut. She would live if she didn't bleed to death.

Just then a horse whinnied shrilly.

Fargo looked over the bank. The outlaws had succeeded in shoving Granger onto his animal and Semple and Hoby had climbed on theirs while Timbre Wilson continued to blast at the posse. Semple's animal had just been hit and was staggering. Quickly, Hoby reined alongside him and Semple sprang from his horse to Hoby's.

"Shoot their animals!" Luther Coltraine bawled. "Don't let them get away!"

Fargo saw a posse member appear and take deliberate aim. But not at the outlaws and their mounts. At the Ovaro.

Fargo shot him. He aimed for the man's arm and winged him and the man stumbled from sight. Launching himself over the bank, Fargo darted to the Ovaro, grabbed the reins, and was in the saddle before anyone could get off a shot. A jab of his spurs and the stallion went over the bank in a flying bound.

Amanda had passed out and was still pumping blood.

Fargo should leave her and fly like the wind, but if he did she might die before the posse found her. Angry at the turn of events, he sprang down, shoved the Henry into the scabbard, lifted the girl, and was in the saddle and away. Crossing the creek, he passed through a stretch of woods to open prairie. Some hills a quarter mile off were the next cover. Lashing the reins, he brought the Ovaro to a gallop.

No one gave chase. No one fired at them.

The marshal and the posse were so intent on the outlaws, they'd forgotten about Amanda and him.

Good, Fargo thought.

The Ovaro reached the hills in under two minutes, but it was two minutes of more blood loss for Amanda, and when they got there, the whole front of her dress was scarlet.

Hastening to a patch of timber, Fargo brought the stallion to a stop and was out of the saddle with the girl in his arms. Setting her down, he hurriedly collected fallen limbs and broke them and got a fire going. The smoke might give them away but he had a graver concern.

Drawing the toothpick, Fargo cut her dress at the shoulder to expose the wound. He was no surgeon; he couldn't go in and tie the vein off. The best he could do was take the unlit end of a burning brand and press the burning end to the bullet hole.

Her flesh sizzled and hissed and she moaned and writhed even though she was out to the world.

Selecting another brand, Fargo did the same to the exit wound. Her blood finally stopped oozing.

Sitting back, Fargo threw the brand away. She might live. She might not. Only the proverbial time would tell. By rights he should take her to town or at the very least hand her over to the posse. Only the posse might shoot him on sight, and in town he'd likely be taken into custody and thrown behind bars again.

Fargo frowned. She needed to be looked after until she recovered enough to get by on her own and there was no one but him handy. As much as he wanted to go after the Cotton Gang and have a talk with Luther Coltraine, he was stuck being nursemaid.

He summed up his sentiments with, "Well, hell."

35

It was pushing midnight when Amanda Brenner opened her eyes.

By then Fargo had found a spring and filled his coffeepot to the brim and washed and cleaned her wounds and bandaged her with strips he cut from the hem of her dress. He'd put coffee on and was seated with the Henry across his lap when she uttered a tiny cry and raised her head.

"Where? What?"

"You're all right, girl," Fargo said. "You were shot but I took care of it."

Amanda looked at the bandage. "You did this for me?" she weakly asked. "I didn't think you liked me much."

Fargo didn't, but he spared her feelings by saying, "I've got more jerky if you're hungry."

"What I am is thirsty," Amanda said. "I'm so parched my throat hurts."

Fargo had filled his canteen at the spring. Uncapping it, he knelt and carefully held it to her lips. She gratefully swallowed and when she had had enough, said, "Thank you."

Fargo checked the bandage for fresh blood but it was dry. Reclaiming his seat, he refilled his tin cup.

"What happened to Luther?"

"I don't know."

"What about Hoby Cotton and the rest of the outlaws?"

"I don't know."

"What *do* you know?"

"I'll take you home as soon as you're up to the ride," Fargo said. It could be a day or two. And they'd have to slip into town late at night in order not to be spotted.

"I want to go now. I want to find Luther and make sure he's all right."

Fargo shook his head.

"Damn you. All that shooting. He could be hurt or dead, even."

"Worry about yourself," Fargo advised. "That shoulder could become infected."

"I don't care about me," Amanda said. "I only care about Luther. You told me you've been in love before. You must know how I feel."

"You're young enough to be his daughter."

"So what? That's something my folks would say. That it's not right, a girl my age. Well, I say love isn't a matter of age. Love is in the heart and the heart is ageless."

"Did you read that in one of your books?"

"No. It's me. It's how I feel. And if I want to go to him, you can't stop me."

"I don't have to," Fargo said. "Your body will stop you for me."

"We'll see about that," Amanda angrily declared. She tried to rise and made it onto an elbow but groaned and sank down again. "My head is spinning. And I feel so weak."

"Told you," Fargo said.

"Consarn it all." Amanda closed her eyes. "I'll rest a while and try again."

Her while turned out to be the whole night. She didn't awaken again until the sun was up. Fargo had managed to get in a few hours himself but he couldn't stop yawning.

"It's morning" were the first words out of her mouth.

"Nothing escapes you, does it?" Fargo said.

"Don't be rude. And I demand once again that you take me back. This afternoon will do. Then I'll be out of your hair and you'll be free to go wherever you please."

"I'm not going anywhere until this is finished."

"Finished how?"

Behind Fargo a gun hammer clicked and a man said, "I'd like to hear the answer to that my own self."

"Luther!" Amanda happily exclaimed.

Fargo didn't lose his head and do something rash. He calmly turned it and said, "Let me guess. It was the smoke."

Luther Coltraine looked the worse for wear. His face and clothes were caked with dust and he needed a shave. His six-shooter leveled unwaveringly at Fargo, he came around and sank to a knee next to Amanda.

"I knew you'd come," Amanda said, tears filling her eyes. "I knew it as true as I know anything."

Luther touched her bandage. "Who shot you? Him?"

"Oh, no. It happened in all that confusion between your posse and the Cotton Gang."

"Where are they, by the way?" Fargo asked.

"Most of the outlaws got away," Coltraine said. "We chased them until after dark and I sent the posse back to town. Our horses were about worn out and the men weren't much better off."

"Why only most?" Fargo said.

"Granger Cotton is dead. We found his body lying on the prairie. He'd been shot in the lungs. My men took the body back with them."

"And your son?"

Coltraine looked at Amanda.

"He knows all of it," she said.

"You didn't."

"Hoby told him," Amanda lied. "About his ma and you. About him following you here. About nearly everything."

"Damn that boy, anyhow," Coltraine said. "He's been a thorn in my side since that day he showed up out of the blue in Texas and informed me he was mine. I told him I didn't want anything to do with him but he keeps makin' my life miserable. I reckon it's his way of payin' me back for that night I spent with his mother."

"He hates you," Fargo said.

"Does he ever," Coltraine said. "Why do you think he followed me here? I left Texas to get away from him and he came after me to plague me like he did there. He didn't rob the Horse Creek bank for the money. He did it to rub my nose in the fact he hates my guts."

"Hoby Cotton is despicable," Amanda said. "You're better off putting an end to him the first chance you get."

"I don't know if I can," Coltraine said quietly. "He's my flesh and blood, after all."

"You hardly know him," Amanda said.

"Doesn't matter. When you have kids of your own someday, you'll understand. I don't want anything to do with him but I can't kill him, either." Coltraine focused on Fargo. "Now then. What to do about you?"

"There's only one thing to do," Amanda said. "Let him go for helping me."

"Can't," Coltraine said. "He shot one of my posse. Two others witnessed it. I'll put him in jail and leave it for a judge to decide."

"He could be sent to prison," Amanda said.

"That's up to the judge."

"The gent I shot was about to shoot my horse," Fargo explained. Not that he should have to make excuses.

"He says it was you he was shooting at."

Amanda surprised Fargo by saying, "It's not fair. I wouldn't be here if not for him. If you love me you'll turn your back so he can ride off."

"You're forgettin' what he said about finishin' this," Coltraine reminded her, and tilted his head quizzically at Fargo. "What did you mean by that, anyhow?"

"Just this," Fargo said, and threw his coffee in Luther Coltraine's face.

36

A bound brought Fargo around the fire. Coltraine was rising and wiping at his eyes with a sleeve. He never saw the uppercut that Fargo let fly. It jolted the lawman onto his bootheels. Fargo went after him, driving a right into Coltraine's gut and a left to the chin.

Most men would have gone down. Not the Texan. Coltraine recovered his wits and his balance and clubbed at Fargo's head with his revolver. Fargo blocked the blow and grabbed Coltraine's wrist, and twisted.

The marshal swore as his six-shooter fell. Wrenching free, he brought up both fists and made the mistake of growling, "I'll beat you to a pulp for that."

They stood toe to toe, slugging. Fargo dodged an overhand and slipped a jab and landed a solid cross. Coltraine caught him on the cheek as he drew back his arm.

Circling, swinging, countering, they fought with increasing savagery. Coltraine seemed determined to batter Fargo into the ground. He was good, too. Any opening Fargo gave him, however slight, Coltraine instantly took advantage of.

Fargo did the same. He opened Coltraine's cheek. He bruised Coltraine's jaw. He landed another punch to Coltraine's gut but it was like hitting a washboard. Fargo wasn't the only one with a lot of muscle packed on his frame.

"Stop it! Please!" Amanda Brenner cried.

Neither of them paid her any mind.

Fargo wasn't going back to jail. He'd do whatever it took to stay free. The lawman was in the wrong, and not to be trusted. His womanizing had been the death of his reputation in Texas. Fargo wasn't about to let it be the death of him.

For minutes that seemed like eternities they battled furiously. Coltraine flicked a boot at Fargo's knee. A dirty move, and Fargo retaliated in kind. Where Coltraine had missed, Fargo didn't. Coltraine grimaced and tottered. Fargo connected with a right cross that should have ended the fight but Coltraine shrugged it off. The man was tough.

They were so intent in beating each other senseless that neither paid much attention to where they stepped. Not until Fargo felt sudden heat and pain and realized they had blundered into the fire.

Coltraine saw it at the same time and leaped back out of reach. Smoke was rising from a boot and he stomped it and swore.

Fargo glanced around to be sure the lawman's fallen six-shooter wasn't in easy reach. He could use his Colt if he wanted but he had started this with his fists and he would end it with them.

"This is what I get for goin' easy on you," the marshal said. "I never should have let you out of jail."

Fargo was grateful for the breather and sought to make it last longer by saying, "What's the real reason you left Texas?"

"I already told you," Coltraine said. "That boy was doin' his damnedest to make my life a livin' hell. Thanks to him, rumors were spreadin'."

"About all the women you'd bedded," Fargo guessed. "Hoby's

ma wasn't the only one." He didn't really think Coltraine would answer, not with Amanda there, but evidently he'd forgotten about her.

"A man has needs. And you have no call to criticize. When it comes to women, I hear tell you put every he-bull around to shame. You can't keep your pecker in your pants any more than I can."

"I don't pretend it's something it isn't," Fargo said. "I never say it's love when it's not."

Coltraine shrugged. "Love talk is like flowers. A man does what he has to to get them to part their legs."

"You hear that, Amanda?" Fargo said.

Amanda had. She has risen on her elbows and looked as if her whole world had come crashing down. "Luther, no," she said softly.

"I've never done that with you, darlin'," Coltraine assured her. "I care for you, gal. You know that."

"Do I?"

"We'll go away together," Coltraine said. "I'll have Fargo thrown in prison and deal with my wretch of a son, and we'll start a new life together."

"Why don't I believe you?" Amanda said.

Coltraine glared at Fargo. "Look at what you've done. Turned her against me."

"For the first time she sees you for how you are."

"All those others meant nothin' to me. She does, I tell you."

"I don't give a damn about any of that," Fargo said. "Give me your word you won't try to arrest me on trumped-up charges and I'll leave you and her to hash it out yourselves."

"No," Amanda said. "I don't want to be alone with him. Now that I know the truth, there's no telling what he might do."

"I'd never harm a hair on your head, gal," Coltraine said. "You mean too much to me."

"Quit lying, Luther," Amanda said sadly.

Coltraine grew red with anger. "And you want me to just let you ride off?" he said to Fargo. "To trust you not to go to the newspapers? If this got out, it'd be the end of my law days. No one would hire me."

"I've already told you I don't care about your womanizing."

"I don't believe you. You'd ruin me if you could, just like Hoby. I can't have that." Coltraine brought his fists up. "You're goin' to prison where you can't do me any harm."

"Over my dead body," Fargo said.

"Whatever it takes," Luther Coltraine said, and came at him anew.

Fargo got his arms up just in time to ward off a blow that would have taken his head off. He jabbed, sidestepped, and hit hard twice to Coltraine's ribs. Coltraine decided to do the same to him and unknowingly caught him on his stab wound. The pain nearly doubled him over.

To hold Coltraine off, Fargo streaked a punch at his face. He missed but it drove the lawman back.

"Luther," Amanda said. "Stop this."

"Go to hell," Coltraine said without looking at her. "You chose to believe him over me."

"I may be young but I'm not stupid," Amanda said. "You've used me like you used those other women. But I suppose it's as much my fault as yours. I threw myself at you, at the great man who could do no wrong." She laughed bitterly.

Coltraine turned his face to her. "What will it take to convince you?"

"Do what's right," Amanda said, "and let him go."

"I can't. I'm sorry."

"Then I'm sorry too," Amanda said. "It's over between us. I'm going to confess everything to my parents and take my medicine and move on with my life."

"You can't do that to me," Coltraine said. "I'll be fired."

"You could go to Denver. I hear they have a lot of houses of ill repute. At least you wouldn't have to lie to get them to shed their clothes for you."

"Oh, Amanda," Coltraine said.

She looked at Fargo and some of her old spirit returned. "Would you do me favor?"

"If I can," Fargo said.

"Beat the hell out of him. I can't do it myself and I want to see this so-and-so bleed."

37

"You little bitch," Luther Coltraine growled.

"So much for true love," Fargo said.

Coltraine glared, then let out a bellow worthy of a bull buffalo and came at Fargo like a madman. His arms pinwheeling, Coltraine sought to overpower him by brute strength.

Countering as best he could, Fargo gave way. Some of the blows connected, provoking spikes of pain. He let them. He blocked, he weaved, but he didn't strike back. It emboldened Coltraine into swinging wilder. Which was exactly what Fargo wanted.

The moment he had been waiting for came. Coltraine cocked his right arm and lowered his left farther than he should've. Fargo tensed, and when the right fist flashed, he shifted to avoid it and slammed his own into Coltraine's jaw with all the force in his sinews.

Luther Coltraine took a single, faltering step, shook his head to try to clear it, and sprawled in a heap in the dust.

"You beat him!" Amanda happily cried, and forgetting her shoulder wound, she clapped her hands.

Fargo stood over the lawman, breathing deeply. His knuckles were bruised and his ribs were on fire.

"Now what?" Amanda asked.

Good question, Fargo thought. "I take you home and you tell your folks about him."

Amanda stared at her lover and gnawed her lip. "They'll be mad as can be but it'll be worth it to see him disgraced. He has it coming for how he treated me and all those other women."

Fargo felt like a bit of a hypocrite. After all, he was fond of the ladies, too. The difference being that he didn't wear a badge and pretend to be a model of virtue. And he wouldn't arrest someone on false grounds to have them thrown in prison. "I suppose he has it coming."

"You *suppose*?" Amanda declared in disbelief. "He deserves it, if anyone does. Help me up and we'll head out."

"I don't think you're strong enough yet."

"Then what are you going to do? Tie him and keep him prisoner until I'm fit to ride?"

"I have an idea," said a new voice. "How about if I take him off your hands?"

Fargo whirled at the "I," and froze.

"Miss me?" Hoby Cotton said with a grin. He was flanked by Semple and Timbre Wilson, both with their six-guns leveled.

"Not you again," Amanda said.

"I'm like a bad penny," Hoby said. "Or so my pa, here, keeps tellin' me." He walked up and jabbed Coltraine with a toe. "How the mighty have fallen. Ain't that how it goes?"

"Where did you come from?" Amanda asked. "I thought you'd be halfway back to Texas by now."

"Not a chance," Hoby said. "Not while there's unfinished business between him and me."

Fargo didn't like the sound of that. "Unfinished how?"

Hoby moved to the fire and squatted and helped himself to Fargo's coffee. "For a long time now I've done all I can to make him a laughingstock. Saved the best for last, robbin' the bank under his nose like I did."

"I'm guessing that's not enough," Fargo said when the boy didn't go on.

"Not by a long shot." Hoby swallowed and smiled. "My ma cheated on her husband for him and he left her in the lurch. When I found out and showed up on his doorstep, did he greet his long-lost son with open arms? He did not. He treated me like dirt and told me to get lost. And now his posse has killed one of my brothers. He has a lot to answer for, has Luther Coltraine."

"What will you do to him?" Amanda asked.

"Might be I'll drag him for a couple of miles over the rockiest parts I can find," Hoby said. "I hear that peels the skin and flesh right off."

"That would be terrible."

"Wouldn't it, though?" Hoby said, and laughed. He drained the tin cup and tossed it away, then stood and stepped to Amanda. Hunkering, he tapped her bandage. "What happened to you?"

"A stray bullet," Amanda said. "I would have died if not for Skye."

"How sweet," Hoby said, and before anyone could guess his intent, he punched the bandage as hard as he could.

122

Amanda screamed.

Fargo took a step but stopped when Timbre Wilson and Semple pointed their revolvers.

"No, you don't, mister," Timbre Wilson said. "We'll shoot you dead if you try to help her."

Clutching herself, Amanda writhed and sobbed. She might have gone on a good while but Hoby lunged and cupped her chin and held her face steady.

"Enough bawlin', bitch. It hurts my ears."

"Why?" Amanda said. "What did I ever do to you?"

"You let him poke you," Hoby said, with a nod at Coltraine. "And when I warned you about him, you wouldn't listen."

"I was in love," Amanda said, wincing. "Or thought I was. Now my eyes have been opened and I see him for how he truly is."

"So you won't care if I flay him to pieces?"

"Flay away," Amanda said. "And when I'm up to it, I'll dance on his grave."

"Good for you," Hoby said. He reached out and she flinched and drew away but all he did was pat her on the head. "I reckon I'm sorry for that wallop."

Fargo had seldom come across anyone so . . . unpredictable. The boy was deadly one minute, friendly the next.

"How about you, scout?" Hoby asked, turning. "Would you butt in if I took a knife and went to slit his throat."

"Coltraine is nothing to me," Fargo said. Although he wouldn't stand there and let it happen.

"Well, then," Hoby said. "We'll take him and be on our way."

"Hold on," Timbre Wilson said. "You're forgettin' about Abe, and how this scout nearly killed me."

"I never forget nothin'," Hoby said. "Semple and me will light out with my so-called pa. You stay and take care of the scout and the girl."

"What?" Amanda said.

"Come now, darlin'," Hoby said. "I let you live, they'd use you against me if they ever brought me to trial. They'd put you on the stand and make you swear on the Bible that the last you saw of the marshal, Semple and me were cartin' him off to send him into the hereafter."

"I'd never do that," Amanda said.

Hoby winked at Fargo. "I should be mad at how dumb folks think I am. But I'm not dumb, am I?"

"No," Fargo said, "dumb is one thing you're not."

Pleased, Hoby beamed. "I'm smart enough to know that you're the only hombre in a hundred miles who could track me and my pards down. Which is extra reason to blow out your wick."

"Why don't I do it and get it over with?" Timbre Wilson said.

"Weren't you sayin' as how you'd love to poke this pretty little filly your own self?" Hoby said. "That it's a shame the marshal was havin' all the fun?"

Timbre stared at Amanda and a lecherous gleam came into his eyes. "I do believe I did."

"There you go." Hoby laughed and said to Semple, "Fetch our horses and our ropes, and let the fun commence."

38

It was becoming a habit. Every time Fargo turned around, he was trussed up like a lamb for slaughter. He should be thankful that Hoby Cotton hadn't simply shot him, but the rope biting into his wrists and legs was a painful harbinger that he didn't have long to live, anyhow.

Timbre Wilson watched the Cottons ride out. Semple led Coltraine's horse, with the lawman facedown over the saddle.

Amanda lay near petrified with fear. She couldn't take her eyes off Wilson. Clearly, she yearned to rise and run but she was still too weak to do more than say, "Lay a hand on me and you'll regret it."

"You don't say," Timbre Wilson replied.

"Violating a woman will get you hung," Amanda tried again.

Timbre glanced at her and licked his lips. "Who's to know? The scout, there, will be rottin' in the dirt. You won't be around, neither."

"I can't believe this is happening," Amanda said. "All because I fell in love."

"What I don't believe in is that," Timbre Wilson said.

"In what?"

"In love, you jackass. It's a fancy word folks use who like to strip bare and go at it. To me a poke is just a poke."

Amanda tried another angle. "You were nice to me once. Back when Hoby took me from the bank."

"I had to be," Timbre said, still watching his friends fade into the far-off haze. "Hoby's orders. He wanted to study on you and said the rest of us were to treat you like we would our own sisters." He chuckled at that.

"Why did he want to study me?"

"He was tryin' to figure you out. He couldn't savvy how you could be so stupid as to give yourself to Coltraine."

"He doesn't believe in love either?"

"The kid? Sure he does. He's not as practical as me. Give him a few years and he'll learn better."

Fargo was trying to slip his fingers into his boot but the rope around his ankles was too tight. He'd have to find another way.

"Now then," Timbre said, turning at last. "I reckon we should get to it." He drew his six-gun. "A pill to the brainpan for him and then you and me will do it until the cows come home."

"I'm not in any shape for that," Amanda said. "I've lost too much blood. All I'd do is lie here."

"So?" Timbre said, and laughed. "That just means you can't scratch my eyes out."

Amanda looked at Fargo. "All I ever wanted was to be happy. Is that too much to ask of life?"

Fargo tensed his legs without being obvious. He'd be damned if he'd go out meekly. He needed Wilson to come a couple of steps closer, though.

"Now that's somethin' you and me have in common, girl," Timbre Wilson was saying. "I like bein' happy, too."

"You just told me that you don't believe in love," Amanda replied. "What else is there that makes someone truly happy?"

"Killin' and stealin'."

"Don't be ridiculous."

"Ain't ever been more serious in my life," Timbre said. "Nothin' makes me happier than killin' someone. Or helpin' myself to a sack full of money."

"You forgot havin' your way with helpless females."

Timbre Wilson took a step toward her. "It ain't smart to provoke me. Make me mad and you'll suffer more."

"The mere touch of you will be suffering enough," Amanda

declared defiantly. "I wouldn't be surprised if it makes me violently ill."

"I'll just wait until you're done bein' sick and start in again."

"And when you do, I'll think of him," Amanda said.

"What?"

"You heard me. When you put your filthy hands on me, I'll shut you out by thinking of Luther and all the wonderful times we've had."

"If you don't beat all."

"That's right," Amanda said. "I'll think of my love for him, and nothing else. You won't exist. Do what you want to me, you animal, and it will be as if I'm not even here."

"Oh, you'll be here, all right," Timbre said, and laughed.

"Shows how much you know," Amanda said. "But then, I doubt you have much of an imagination. Dullards usually don't."

"Quit insultin' me."

"Does it hurt your feelings? You don't like being reminded that you're as intelligent as a tree stump?"

"I'm warnin' you."

"You see me quaking, don't you?" Amanda sarcastically retorted. "Hoby wants to make a laughingstock of Luther but you're the real laughingstock. Why, I bet you can't make love half as good as Luther does."

"Don't you . . ." Timbre Wilson growled, and he was red in the face.

Amanda went on raking her verbal claws. "What's the matter? Afraid I'll compare you to a real man? When you pull down your britches, I'll laugh at how puny you are."

Wilson took another step. He was so mad, he'd forgotten about Fargo. "One more insult, bitch. Just one."

"And what? You'll shoot me and deprive yourself of all that fun? Just because you're afraid I'll remind you that you're not much where it really counts?"

"That does it."

Fargo was ready. When Timbre Wilson took another step and raised his six-shooter to club her, he exploded into motion. He rammed both feet against Wilson's left knee and there was a sharp *crack*.

Wilson cried out and his leg buckled and he pitched forward, almost on top of Amanda. Instantly, he twisted and went to point his revolver at Fargo.

Shrieking like a banshee, Amanda Brenner flung herself at the outlaw. She wasn't as weak as she'd let on. Her hand streaked, her fingernails digging deep. She'd gone for one of his eyes.

A howl tore from Timbre Wilson's throat. He threw himself back, or tried to.

Fargo kicked him in the head. He didn't hold back. It was kill or be killed. Wilson fell prone but he didn't lose his hold on the revolver and he snapped off a shot.

Maybe it was the blood welling in one eye or the blow to the head, but Timbre Wilson did something he probably hadn't done at that range since he was old enough to pick up a pistol: he missed.

Snapping his legs as high as they would go, Fargo brought his heels, and his spurs, smashing down onto Wilson's gun hand.

Timbre screamed in rage. He jerked his hand away and grabbed at the revolver with his other hand and sought to rise.

Fargo couldn't let him. Once the outlaw was up and out of reach, it was over. He drove his boots at Timbre's face but Timbre shifted and his boots glanced off the man's shoulder.

In doing so, Wilson put himself closer to Amanda. She struck again, at his other eye, trying to blind him.

Fargo had to hand it to her. She knew just what to do. But this time she missed and Timbre Wilson clubbed her.

"And now for you, scout!" the outlaw cried.

39

Fargo had already raised his legs high, and as Timbre Wilson trained the six-gun on him, he arced his spurs into Wilson's neck. His spurs didn't have long rowels but like most they came to points and those points were sharp enough to pierce flesh. He went for the jugular, not really expecting to stab deep enough to cause Wilson any great harm.

Again Wilson screamed, but this time not from rage. A red mist sprayed from his neck, turning into a rain of scarlet drops and then a fountain. Dropping his revolver, he clutched at his throat with both hands.

Fargo didn't give him a moment's respite. His spurs had proven effective twice. Why not a third time? He speared his legs at Wilson's temple. To his surprise, his spurs not only imbedded themselves, they stuck fast.

Timbre Wilson cursed mightily and let go of his throat to push at Fargo's legs. Blood poured from the severed vein, a river of red that spread across the outlaw's chest, soaking his shirt.

Fargo pulled his legs back to kick again but it wasn't necessary.

Wilson broke into convulsions. Mewing like a stricken cat, he thrashed and kicked and bucked and finally let out a gurgling cry that ended with him going stiff and then limp and unmoving.

For long seconds Fargo and Amanda Brenner stared, until she anxiously asked, "Is he . . . ?"

Fargo nudged the outlaw's shoulder. When there was no reaction, he kicked harder. Wilson's head rolled in his direction and he found himself gazing into a pair of glazing eyes gone wide with shock. "He's done for."

"Thank God."

"You did good, girl," Fargo complimented her.

"It was you who did him in," Amanda said. "I've never seen spurs used that way. You're awful resourceful."

"I like breathing," Fargo said, and wriggled his forearms. "When you're up to it, untie me."

She pried and pried but the knots were tight, and she had to stop and rest before she could try again.

"I'm sorry. I'm still not myself."

"There's no hurry," Fargo lied. The longer they took, the less chance he had of pulling Marshal Luther Coltraine's fat out of the fire of vengeance of his unforgiving son.

Amanda wasn't fooled. "Yes, there certainly is," she replied. "There's Luther to think of."

It took much too long. Over an hour, and when the last knot parted, she sank down saying, "I can barely keep awake."

Fargo was worried about her blood loss. To say nothing of infection. She needed a sawbones. He reclaimed his Colt and Henry and went to her to lift her onto Wilson's mount, only to find she had passed out.

That clinched it. She was in no condition to ride.

Fargo managed to climb on the Ovaro while holding onto her,

and once they were settled in the saddle, he brought the stallion to a trot. They had a long ways to go and weren't halfway there when she groaned and stirred and drowsily raised her head.

"What? Where?"

"You're safe," Fargo said. "I have you."

Amanda looked around. "How far behind them are we?"

"Far enough."

She squinted at the sun and looked around again. "Wait. Hoby and his brother headed south. But we're not, are we?"

"No," Fargo admitted.

"You're taking me to Horse Creek."

"You come first."

Amanda tried to twist to face him but he held her firm. "Consarn you, no. It's not right we let them kill him. No matter what he's done."

Fargo didn't answer.

"Please. For my sake."

"No."

"Need I remind you I tried to have you killed? I sent you into that ambush at the sodbuster's, remember? You don't owe me a thing."

"Which reminds me," Fargo said. "I've been meaning to ask. Who did you do it for? Coltraine or Hoby Cotton?"

"I did it on my own."

"Liar."

Amanda was quiet a while, then said, "Luther was worried you'd uncover the truth about his son. He couldn't have that get out. Folks would think poorly of him, and he might have lost his job. So I set things up with Hoby, who was still acting sweet to me then."

"I reckoned as much."

"Oh, you know everything, don't you? I could have refused. But I loved Luther so much, I didn't care what happened to you. So you see, your concern is misplaced. Forget about me and go after the Cottons."

"Nice try."

"I hate you," Amanda spat.

Fargo laughed.

The sun was setting when the silhouettes of buildings lined the horizon. Fargo approached with caution. The locals wouldn't hesitate to shoot him on sight. He entered the town by way of a narrow side street. A junction brought him to the rear of the jail.

Amanda had passed out again.

Holding her in place, Fargo slid off, then carefully lowered her and carried her to the back door. He used a thumb on the latch and strode in making no attempt at stealth.

Deputy Wilkins was at the desk, scribbling something. The tip of his tongue poked from his mouth and he was a study in concentration. On hearing Fargo's footfalls, he turned and started to smile. "Marshal, is that you?"

"Here," Fargo said, walking over. "She's all yours."

"What?" Wilkins blurted. He was so surprised that, without thinking, he stood and held out his arms to take her. "What's going on? Where's the marshal?"

Fargo let go of Amanda and stepped back. "She needs a doctor right away or she could die."

"Wait. I'm supposed to arrest you for kidnappin'—" Wilkins stopped and looked at Amanda. "But if you've brought her back, then I guess I shouldn't. I wish the marshal was here. I'm sort of confused."

"She'll enlighten you."

"Hold on. You haven't said about Marshal Coltraine. Why isn't he with you? Did he tell you to bring her back alone?"

"I'm here, aren't I?"

"What does he want me to do? Form another posse and you'll take me to him?"

"You're to stay here." Fargo reached the cells and said over his shoulder, "You'll make a better marshal than Coltraine did."

"That's plumb silly. He's smarter and braver than I can ever be. I could never take his place."

"Don't sell yourself short. There's one thing you do that he never could."

"What's that?" Deputy Wilkins asked.

"You keep your pecker in your pants."

40

Fargo made camp out on the prairie. Some of the good citizens of Horse Creek might still blame him for shooting one of their own during the skirmish with the outlaws, and he didn't care to be strung up by a lynch mob.

He slept soundly and was in the saddle at the crack of dawn. He reasoned that since the Cottons had headed south, he might strike their trail if he rode due east far enough. By his reckoning he shouldn't have to go more than ten or twelve miles.

He hadn't gone more than five when Nature reared her temperamental head.

A storm front swept in and for more than six hours a steady rain fell. Any hope of tracking the Cottons and their captive was lost.

Fargo didn't give up. He counted on sooner or later coming across their sign or spotting smoke from their campfire.

Two days went by with him the sole speck of human life in a vast sea of grass.

The morning of the third day, Fargo crested a rise and spied gray wisps rising from low hills. It could be anyone, including hostiles, but he had high hopes.

In case it was a war party he approached from downwind. Their horses might catch the Ovaro's scent and act up and give him away.

The heat of summer had browned the grass and the wildflowers were wilted.

Buffalo wallows testified to a large herd that had gone by recently. Flies were thick in the wallows, drawn by the urine mixed with the dirt.

When Fargo judged that his quarry was just over the next hill, he drew rein and swung down. Taking the Henry, he climbed. Below the crown he flattened and removed his hat.

It was the Cottons, sure enough. They had a fire going, and Semple was relaxing and drinking coffee.

Not Hoby. The boy-man was pacing and kept glancing to the north.

Fargo knew why. Timbre Wilson was overdue. They'd expected him to overtake them by now.

Marshal Luther Coltraine was trussed from his shoulders to his ankles with rope. He'd been gagged, as well. His hat was gone and his gun belt, too.

Fargo craned his head to hear better.

"—give him another day," Semple was saying. "You know how he is. He'd poke her until he couldn't poke anymore."

"It's been too long, I tell you," Hoby said.

"What do you want to do, then?" Semple asked. "Keep goin'? It'll take Timbre even longer to find us."

"Don't I know that?" Hoby snapped. He did more pacing and rubbed his chin. "I have half a mind to turn back."

"It's your decision but I think you're worried over nothin'. Timbre can take care of himself."

"We should have stayed. That scout is a tricky cuss."

"What could he do, tied like he was?"

"I don't know." Hoby suddenly stopped and walked over to the marshal. Squatting, he tugged the gag free. "How are you holdin' up, Pa?"

"Go to hell," Luther Coltraine said.

Hoby laughed. "Is that any way to talk to your own flesh and blood? The least you can do is be polite."

"If you thought highly of bein' my son, you wouldn't be doin' this."

"Highly?" Hoby said, raising his voice. "Why, you rotten bastard. You abandoned me all those years and you expect me to think highly of you?"

"I didn't know your ma got pregnant," Coltraine said. "I had her that one night and moved on."

"That one night," Hoby said.

"Grow up," Coltraine said angrily. "Men sleep with women all the time and go their separate ways, and that's that. You might have done it yourself, even as young as you are."

"She was a married lady."

"She didn't act married," Coltraine said. "God's own truth, boy, she threw herself at me. I hadn't known her an hour and she was peelin' her clothes off."

"Keep talkin'," Hoby said.

"What is there to say? She had a hankerin' and I wanted to, and we did it. And the next mornin' I rode off and never heard from her again. If she'd written me that she was with child, I'd have gone back."

"Like hell you would. What did you care? She had a husband. You'd have let them raise me."

"Better them than me," Coltraine said. "I wasn't fit to be a father. Hell, I'm still not."

"At last somethin' we agree on."

Coltraine seemed to study his son. "Why do you hate me so much? Because I wasn't there for you when you were growin' up? The man who did raise you, Sam Cotton, wasn't he a good pa?"

"He thought I was his own and treated me as such," Hoby said. "When I turned bad, as folks call it, he didn't know what to do. He figured I'd change my wild ways if he went on showin' how much he cared. But I like the wild ways too much to ever give them up." Hoby paused. "Poor Sam never suspected my blood was tainted."

"Tainted how?" Coltraine asked.

"With yours."

Coltraine struggled to rise on an elbow. "You can't blame how you are on me. I'm as law-abidin' as they come. I've worn a tin star for pretty near twenty years."

"And how many women have you poked in that time?"

"Pokin' females isn't a crime, boy. It's a need like eatin' and sleepin'."

"Is that a fact?" Hoby said, standing. "I have needs, too. Do you know what one of mine is?" Without warning he kicked Coltraine in the chest. "I feel a need to hurt and to kill. It just comes over me and there's nothin' I can do. Like the need I'm feelin' now about you."

Fargo pressed the Henry to his shoulder. The moment had come. He didn't like Luther Coltraine but he wouldn't let the boy murder him. He pressed his cheek to the brass receiver.

"Up there!" Semple Cotton suddenly bellowed, pointing. "It's the scout!"

Fargo went to fix a bead but Hoby Cotton spun and drew with lightning speed and fired twice from the hip. Fargo dropped flat and it was well he did. The slugs whistled narrowly over his head. He rose to shoot but now Semple and Hoby both fired and again he was forced to flatten. More shots boomed, kicking miniature geysers from the hill.

A horse whinnied and hooves pounded, and Fargo heaved up yet again. The Cottons were racing to the south, and each had swung onto the off-side of their mount, Comanche-fashion. He aimed at Hoby's horse but hesitated. He never killed a horse if he could help it. The hesitation proved costly as the pair galloped around the next hill and were gone.

Jamming his hat on, Fargo descended to the Ovaro, shoved the Henry in the scabbard, and led the stallion to the fire.

"Thank God," Luther Coltraine said. "I'm obliged for the rescue."

"Are you?" Fargo squatted and lifted the coffeepot. It was half-full. He got his cup and filled it.

Coltraine was gaping. "What in hell are you doin'. Cut me free so we can go after them."

"Soon enough."

"They'll get away."

"No," Fargo said. "They won't."

Coltraine's jaw muscles twitched. "What are you playin' at? Is this your way of gettin' back at me for that prison business? Untie me, damn you, or there will be hell to pay."

"There will be anyway," Fargo said. "This isn't over until the Cottons are dead. Or we are."

41

Fargo let the famous lawman stew half an hour. By then the Ovaro was rested enough. Drawing the toothpick, he went over and with two quick slashes, cut the ropes.

Luther Coltraine angrily tried to push to his feet but his circulation had been cut off so long that he was only halfway up when his limbs gave out and he collapsed again.

"Damn you, anyway."

"You're welcome to go after them yourself."

"If I knew for a fact he was leavin' the territory and wouldn't ever bother me again, I wouldn't go after him at all," Coltraine said.

"And forget all those he'd killed and robbed?"

"He's my son."

"Which hasn't mattered much."

"Go to hell."

On that cheerful note another twenty minutes elapsed before Coltraine recovered enough to stand and work his arms and legs back and forth. "I'm ready," he announced, "and I'd be grateful if you shared a firearm. The boy took my six-shooter."

"When the time comes," Fargo said.

"I could demand you hand your rifle or pistol over."

"You could try."

Coltraine was sullen when they mounted and became more so as they rode. He didn't speak unless spoken to, and he glared a lot.

Fargo was past caring. He wanted to end it and get on with his life. He'd lost all respect for Coltraine, but at the same time, he doubted the lawman would jump him when his back was turned. The man had some dignity left.

The Cottons had ridden hard and left plenty of tracks. They were making a beeline due south.

"You'd think they were headin' for Texas," Coltraine broke his long sulk. "If only I were that lucky."

"They won't reach it," Fargo said.

Coltraine grew thoughtful. "You do know I'm exceedin' my authority? I'm the town marshal. I have no jurisdiction this far from Horse Creek."

"You have the right to go after lawbreakers."

"It just seems strange. Him my blood and all. I wish his ma never got pregnant. Then none of this would have happened."

"What if you'd gotten Amanda pregnant?" Fargo was curious. "Would you have done the right thing or left her to fend for herself?"

"She's special."

"Aren't they all? And you didn't answer me."

"Not that I have to," Coltraine said, "but I can't really say what I'd do. I wouldn't make up my mind until I had to."

"You'd leave her," Fargo predicted. "I can't see you tying yourself to one woman for the rest of your life."

"Who are you to judge?"

"You have a point," Fargo conceded. "I used to think we were alike, you and me. We both are fond of a roll in the hay. But I don't build myself up in their eyes to get up their dress and then tell them lies until I'm tired of poking them and the next pretty filly takes my fancy."

"That's harsh. Yes, it could be I've trifled with a few. Every man does."

A thought struck Fargo and it jarred him that he hadn't seen it sooner. "Hoby's ma was young when you met her, wasn't she? About Amanda's age, I reckon."

"A little older. She'd already had two kids. So what?"

"So I'm wondering if they're all young. If the one before Amanda and the one before her were any older."

"We're through talkin' about me."

That they were. Fargo had learned enough. Plus, the tracks showed that the Cottons had slowed and weren't that far ahead.

They came on buffalo sign. A lot of it. Fargo figured it was the same herd as before, and it wasn't until they'd gone a mile or so that it hit him what Hoby was doing. "That boy of yours is damned clever."

"How so?"

"He's following this herd," Fargo said, "so their tracks blend in with those of the buffalo. Right now the tracks are fresh and it's easy to tell them apart. But anyone coming along in a day or two wouldn't notice a few shod tracks mixed in with so many others."

"I never heard of that trick."

It made Fargo wonder what else the boy might have up his sleeve.

The droppings they came on grew fresher. Fargo estimated they weren't more than an hour behind the buffs when the sun began to dip below the western horizon, transforming the blue of the sky into bands of red and yellow and orange.

"We'll make camp for the night and hit them early in the morning," Fargo announced.

"I'm not tired," Coltraine said. "The sooner we end it, the better."

"If you want to try to sneak up on that clever son of yours in the dark, go right ahead," Fargo said. "I prefer daylight."

"I see what you're sayin'," Coltraine said. "He's liable to rig their blankets so it seems they're sleepin', and when we get close enough, they cut loose."

"That would be one way."

"Hell. I want this over with."

No less than Fargo did. But he stopped in the lee of a hill that would shield them from most of the night wind, and spread out his bedroll. He didn't bother with a fire. Not this close.

Luther Coltraine was a bulky shadow in the darkness, propped on his saddle. "It's funny how life works out."

Fargo grunted.

"Here I am after a son I didn't know I had until he showed up on my doorstep fifteen years after he was born, and who hates me just the same for not being there when he was growin' up. A son who's done his damnedest to make my life a hell."

"If you're fishing for pity, you're in the wrong lake," Fargo said.

"I'm just sayin' it's not fair. I didn't do anything wrong and I'm bein' treated like I did."

"If you start to cry, you can move your blankets somewhere else."

The dark shape of Coltraine's head swung toward him. "You're a hard man, mister. You have no pity in you whatsoever."

"I pity people burned in fires or massacred by hostiles or who have to watch loved ones die of disease. I don't pity grown men who poke every young gal they come across and then whine about it when their poking catches up to them."

"I should have left you behind bars." Coltraine turned and lay on his side with his back to Fargo. "I'm done tryin' to talk to you."

"Good," Fargo said. He stayed up a while, listening to the sounds of the night: the wind, the coyotes, an owl, and once, the distant howl of a wolf. He searched for the twinkling pinpoint of a fire but the Cottons had likely made a cold camp, too.

He slept with his Colt in his hand. A disturbed sleep, where the slightest of sounds woke him. Toward daybreak it was the screech of a cougar. Since it was only half an hour or so until sunrise, he stayed up.

He had to rouse Coltraine. The lawman slept like a log and woke surly.

They saddled up and resumed their hunt as the blazing arc of the sun lit the eastern horizon. Gradually the stars were eclipsed by the brightening sky and the temperature commenced its inevitable climb.

Along about the middle of the morning they came to an especially flat stretch of prairie, and Fargo drew rein.

"What's the matter?" Coltraine asked, following suit. "Why did you stop?"

Fargo pointed.

A mile or so off were a pair of stick figures on horseback.

42

"It's them!" the lawman exclaimed. And with hard jabs of his spurs, he flew in pursuit.

"Don't!" Fargo hollered, but he was wasting his breath. Swearing, he brought the Ovaro to a trot. He would have thought Coltraine had more brains than to pull a stunt like this. The Cottons were bound to hear him and use their own spurs and leave him in the dust.

Coltraine had to know that, which made Fargo wonder if he was doing it deliberately.

The Cottons were oblivious but not for long. One of the stick figures shifted in the saddle and pointed a stick arm. The next moment the pair was off like twin shots.

The chase lasted another mile.

That was when the heat haze gave the illusion that the brown grass of the prairie had darkened and come alive. The grass seemed to grow and swell and resolved into a moving sea of humped forms.

The buffalo were on the move. Numbering in the thousands, the herd tromped a half-mile swath. It was a great living river of horned and hairy brutes that as yet wasn't aware that two riders were racing for that river as if their lives depended on it.

Madness, some would call it. To ride into a herd of buffalo was to court death. But there was a purpose to the madness, a purpose that might enable the Cottons to get away.

If Coltraine didn't see it, Fargo did. He held the Ovaro to a trot, saving the stallion for when he would need its fleetness more. Up ahead, the lawman lashed his reins and slapped his legs, being as foolish as could be. Or was he? Coltraine wasn't stupid. Maybe, just maybe, Coltraine blundered in going after them too soon in order to give Hoby a chance to escape. Preposterous, yes, but possible.

A few of the herd's stragglers had stopped and looked back. They'd heard the Cottons but didn't perceive them as a threat, yet.

Sunlight gleamed on gun barrels. Hoby and Semple had drawn their six-shooters and were waving them over their heads.

Fargo heard whoops and hollers and then the crack of shots, four, five, six.

The buffalo lumbered into motion. Like a gigantic wave driven toward a sandy shore, thousands of dark forms broke into a run almost as one. Thunder rumbled, the pounding of all those hooves driven by tons of muscle into a flowing mass of horn and hair.

And right behind them came the Cottons.

So many buffs, moving so fast, raised a lot of dust. An enormous cloud as wide as the herd and as thick as the thickest fog. A cloud that swallowed Hoby and Semple, as Hoby had planned.

Coltraine still hadn't slowed. He was lashing his mount to renewed effort but the horse was doing its utmost.

It took some tugging for Fargo to pull the red bandana from around his neck up over his mouth and nose. The bandana wouldn't keep out all the dust but it would help.

Coltraine was almost to the cloud and hunched over his saddle, as if that would help.

Fargo was a couple of hundred yards back when the lawman plunged into the dust. Unwilling to make the same mistake, Fargo slowed.

Dust didn't burn the eyes and the throat like smoke but it got into every fold and gap on the human body. Into the eyes, into the nose, into the mouth, and under one's clothes. It was just as bad for a horse. He'd have to check the Ovaro's eyes and nose, after.

One moment Fargo was in bright sunshine, the next he was breathing grit and his eyes felt as if they were being rubbed by sandpaper. He squinted, which made it harder for him to see. He'd lost sight of Coltraine but figured the marshal was still heading south. But was that what the Cottons would do?

Fargo put himself in Hoby's boots. It would occur to the boy that they could slip to the west or east and get clean away. Continuing after the herd was too dangerous. They never knew but when a buffalo might stop and turn at bay.

To the east was more flat but to the west were hills.

Fargo reined west, the dust so heavy, it made him cough. He jerked his hat brim lower in a vain effort to keep it out of his face.

Suddenly a dark shape. Fargo wrenched on the reins and barely missed colliding with a bull buff standing with its legs spread. As he raced by, the bull bellowed and whirled and came after him.

Just what Fargo needed. He was glad he'd conserved the Ovaro because they needed the extra burst of going from a trot to a gallop. Grunting and snorting, the bull sought to overtake them.

One look back was enough. The flaring nostrils and rage-filled eyes left no doubt as to the bull's intentions. A single sweep of those curved horns and the Ovaro would be disemboweled, as many a warrior had found out to their dismay.

Fargo whipped his reins, but sparingly. The stallion knew what to do. They'd been in tights like this before. Too many of them. So what if life on the frontier was by its nature fraught with perils? There came a time when anyone with common sense would say "Enough is enough."

The bull was gaining. Twice it swiped at the Ovaro's hind legs and each time missed by a whisker.

Fargo reined sharply to the right and the bull veered after them. He reined to the left and the bull never missed a stride. The buff was glued to the Ovaro like death itself. All it would take was for the stallion to stumble.

Fargo couldn't take that chance. Drawing his Colt, he pointed it at the bull. It would take a lucky shot to bring the animal down and he wasn't going to try. He needed only to slow it enough that the Ovaro could escape.

A buffalo's skull was inches high. A heavy caliber rifle like a Sharps could penetrate to the brain but Fargo had given up using a Sharps in favor of the Henry and, at moments like this, regretted it.

He aimed at the horns where they grew out of the bull's wide brow. Holding the Colt steady was next to impossible. He did the best he could, and fired.

The bull staggered and slowed but only for an instant. Then it was after them again, vengeance incarnate.

Fargo kept hoping the dust would thin. He was coughing nonstop and his eyes were watering.

The bull bellowed. It had regained half the ground it lost and was rapidly bearing down.

Fargo snapped another shot, then concentrated on riding and on looking for a glimpse of the terrain ahead. The hills might prove a haven if he could reach them.

Suddenly the bull found a reserve of speed. It came alongside the Ovaro and hooked a horn to rip.

43

Fargo hauled on the reins and swerved away and the bull swerved with them. He reined sharply right and then left and the buff stayed by the Ovaro's side. The tip of a horn almost nicked the stallion's belly.

The bull drew back its head to swing again.

Forever after, Fargo wasn't entirely sure what happened next. He suspected that the bull stepped into a prairie dog hole or a cleft. For suddenly it pitched nose-first to the earth and went into a tumble of legs and tail.

Fargo glanced back and saw it on its side, thrashing. Then the dust closed over it. He rode until the choking cloud gave way to clear air and a blue vault overhead.

Still coughing, Fargo came to a stop. The Ovaro was wheezing as if it had run fifty miles and was lathered with dust-colored sweat.

"We did it, big fella," Fargo said, and patted the stallion's neck.

From out of the cloud came another bellow.

Deeming it prudent not to stick around, Fargo turned to the south. He hadn't gone far when he struck the trail of two shod horses. The Cottons. His hunch had paid off.

Fargo rose in the stirrups but didn't spot them. If he was Hoby, he'd have gone into the hills. It could be they were looking for Coltraine.

As for the herd, it was miles away by now. The buffalo would run until exhaustion put an end to their flight. They'd spend the rest of the day grazing and recovering and move on when they felt like it.

Fargo wasn't in any hurry. He aimed to let the Cottons get farther ahead and when dark fell, move in. For once he would spring a surprise and not the other way around.

Twice, Fargo stopped for short spells. The first time was to let the Ovaro rest. The second was so he didn't overtake the Cottons, who weren't that far ahead.

With the thinning of the dust, he spotted buffalo now and then.

Old bulls or cows that couldn't keep up with the herd. Once it was a calf, separated from its mother, bawling and bawling.

The afternoon was an oven. His buckskins clung to him, soaked with his sweat.

It was an hour or more until sunset when he came abreast of a dry wash, and out of it came a horse and rider. His hand was on his Colt before he realized who it was.

"Where have you been?" Luther Coltraine asked. "I've been waitin' forever."

He was caked with dust from hat to boots and his black horse was practically gray.

"Were you hiding from the buffalo?" Fargo said with a bob of his head at the wash.

"I've been followin' the Cottons. I caught sight of them up yonder and hid so they wouldn't spot me."

That made sense, except for one thing. "I thought you were hell-bent for leather to catch them."

"I am," Coltraine said. "But I'm not goin' to ride into their gun sights."

That made sense too, but Fargo couldn't help saying, "You gave us away when you shouldn't have. If you ask me, you're half hoping Hoby won't be caught."

"Don't be ridiculous. He's a lawbreaker. And whatever else folks might say about me, I uphold the law the best I can."

Fargo granted him that, and dropped the subject. But as they rode he pondered, and made a decision that from then on out, he wouldn't turn his back on Coltraine if he could help it.

Presently evening fell and twilight spread and a canopy of stars appeared.

Fargo reckoned that the Cottons would make another cold camp but he reckoned wrong.

"A fire," the marshal declared, pointing. "We've got them now, by God."

It was half a mile off, a lone beacon of flame in the vast ocean of black night.

"Mighty careless of them," Coltraine commented.

"Too careless," Fargo said.

"You reckon it's another of the boy's tricks?"

"What else?" Fargo said. Hoby wouldn't kindle a fire unless he knew he was safe, which he knew he wasn't. Therefore, the fire served another purpose: to lure them in so Hoby could drop them dead with lead.

"I hope it is a trick," Coltraine said. "We can turn the tables and put that boy down like we would a rabid wolf."

"You've changed your mind about shooting your own son?"

"I'd shoot my own ma if she did the things he's done. The killin' and the robbin' has to end. Too many folks have suffered on account of him. Son or not, Hoby Cotton must die."

"And then what?" Fargo asked. "Back to Horse Creek and Amanda Brenner?"

"She doesn't want me anymore. She's made that plain enough." Coltraine sighed. "I reckon I'll head to Texas and take up where I left off when the boy came along to spoil things."

"And no one will ever know he was your son, or any of the rest of it."

"What business is it of anyone but me and his ma? And she's passed on, God rest her soul."

"Convenient," Fargo said.

Coltraine looked at him, his face a dark shadow. "Who are you to judge?"

"I have no call to at all," Fargo agreed.

"I just want to live like I used to," Coltraine said. "I left Texas so I wouldn't have to go up against him. But he came after me. I'll never know peace so long as he's alive."

"I thought you left so he wouldn't ruin your reputation."

"Could be that was part of it. Mostly I was in shock. I'd found out I had a son who was as vicious as can be, and he turned that viciousness on me and those around me so I got out of there. I figured he'd never find me. I was wrong."

Fargo didn't say anything.

"My life has become a mess, and all because I couldn't bring myself to shoot a boy I didn't know I had. I was weak when I shouldn't have been."

"Maybe it wasn't a weakness," Fargo said.

"Whatever it was, I'm done holdin' back. From here on out it's do or die."

44

A stand of trees accounted for the wood for the fire. But the fire wasn't in the trees where it should be, concealed from unfriendly eyes. It was out in the open, a flame to lure in moths.

The Cottons had stripped their mounts and set their saddles near the fire and unwrapped their bedrolls, and from a distance it looked as if the pair was under their blankets and bedded down for the night.

"I expected better of the boy," Luther Coltraine said. "He's graspin' at straws if he reckons this will work."

"He figures you'll take the bait, anyway."

They climbed down and let their reins dangle and advanced on foot, unlimbering their six-shooters as they went.

"Hoby is mine," Coltraine whispered. "You take Semple."

"No promises," Fargo said.

"If you can, do it for me."

The night was still save for a breeze that rustled the leaves on the trees, and the dancing flames.

Fargo was forty yards out when he abruptly stopped. He'd realized something important. "Hold on," he whispered.

"What is it?"

"Where are their horses?"

By rights the animals should be hobbled close by. It was what anyone with a lick of common sense would do. But Fargo hated to take anything for granted where Hoby Cotton was concerned. He hunkered to wait and listen.

Luther Coltraine did the same. "Their animals must be in the trees."

That was the obvious place to hide them but Hoby Cotton never did the obvious. Fargo stared at the saddles and the blankets and the fire, and the seed of an idea took root. "I'll be damned."

"What's wrong?"

Acting on his hunch, Fargo rose and strode boldly into the circle of firelight. No shots rang out. No one yelled for him to drop his six-shooter.

The marshal overtook him, saying, "What's gotten into you? Are you tryin' to get yourself killed?"

Fargo walked up to a blanket and kicked it. Underneath were tree branches and brush to give the illusion of a sleeper.

Coltraine was looking every which way, his Colt leveled. "They probably have their gun sights on us."

"Notice anything?"

"What do you mean?" Coltraine asked while still glancing right and left.

"No rifles. No saddlebags, either."

"What?"

"Just their bedrolls and saddles."

"What?" Coltraine said again. He moved to the other saddle and bent. "Then this wasn't an ambush."

"Hoby rigged it to delay us. He probably hoped we'd wait until daylight to move in."

"And by then him and his brother would be halfway to Texas."

Fargo grinned. "Not quite that far."

Luther Coltraine swore and sent the other blanket flying with a sweep of his leg. "The boy did it to me again."

"To both of us."

"Is that supposed to make me feel better?" Coltraine turned to the south and took a few steps. "His plan didn't work, though. We didn't wait." He jammed his Colt into his holster. "They can't have gotten far. I say we light out after them. We do it careful, we can give that boy a taste of his own medicine."

"We could just as well lose them," Fargo pointed out. And picking up their trail again, come daylight, could prove daunting.

"I'm willin' to try."

Against his better judgment, Fargo gave in. They hurried to their mounts, swung wide of the campfire, and rode at a walk. Any faster, and the sound would give them away.

"At last," Coltraine crowed. "Hoby isn't half as slick as he thinks he is."

Fargo thought the lawman was putting the cart before the horse but he held his peace and strained his ears to catch the faint thud of hooves.

At night the prairie was a sea of sameness, the flats broken here and there by the roll of grassy swells. It gave the illusion it could go on forever. Except for the occasional bleat of a startled deer or the cry of a rabbit in its death throes, an unusual stillness prevailed.

Or it did, until Luther Coltraine cleared his throat.

"I've been thinkin'."

"Good for you."

"Maybe it's time I found a woman I can settle down with and raise a passel of kids of our own."

"Why are you telling me this?"

"I don't know," Coltraine said. "After all we've been through the past few days, you're the closest thing to a friend I've got."

Fargo almost felt sorry for him. Almost. "There's always Amanda."

"By good I mean older."

"You'd give up the young ones?"

"I can try," Coltraine said, not sounding enthusiastic. "I'm almost at the age where they won't be much interested, anyway." He seemed to shake himself. "Yes, sir. Once Hoby is out of the way, I can get on with my life. No more runnin' from my mistakes. I can be a whole new man."

Fargo was about to tell him that they should keep quiet when the stillness was shattered by the blast of gunfire.

45

Luther Coltraine cried out.

The firing came from two points. Fargo saw the muzzle flashes and realized that, once again, Hoby Cotton had outsmarted them. The boy hadn't expected them to wait until morning. Hoby had rightly figured they'd be too eager to wait, and he and his brother had taken positions where anyone heading south from the campfire was bound to run into them.

Hauling on the reins, Fargo got out of there. One of the rifles spanged and a hornet buzzed his ear. For shooting in the dark it was either considerable luck or the shooter was a marksman.

The other rifle was banging, too, and Fargo heard a high whinny from Coltraine's horse and a curse and the crash of the lawman's mount.

Worried sick the same would happen to the Ovaro, Fargo didn't stop. But no lead was sent his way. He went over a hundred yards, far enough to convince himself the Cottons had lost track of him in the dark.

Vaulting down, Fargo crouched and quickly removed his spurs. He wasn't taking any chances they would give him away. Sliding them into a saddlebag, he drew his Colt and hurried toward where he had last seen Coltraine. He heard the lawman swearing, and slowed.

Hoby Cotton's laugh was as cold as ever. "Looks as if the scout ran out on you, Pa."

Fargo froze. The voice wasn't a stone's throw off. He struggled to pierce the murk and distinguished two standing figures and a bulk on the ground.

"And here you are, tin star," Semple Cotton said, chuckling, "pinned by your own critter. Ain't life grand?"

Fargo edged forward.

"Get it over with, damn your hides," Luther Coltraine growled.

"What's the rush?" Hoby replied. "I have you right where I want you and I aim to make the most of it."

"The scout might come back," Semple said.

"I won't have my fun spoiled, by him or anyone else," Hoby said. "Go have a look-see. Make sure he skedaddled."

Fargo crouched.

One of the figures started to the north. "Don't finish the law dog off until I get back. I want to see it."

"Don't you worry none," Hoby said. "I aim to take my sweet time. He'll blubber like a baby before I'm done."

"Like hell I will," Coltraine said.

There was the sound of a blow.

Fargo didn't take his eyes off Semple. The outlaw was coming straight toward him. His thumb on the Colt's hammer, he let Semple get almost on top of him. "That's far enough."

Semple Cotton drew up short. "Well, I'll be. I didn't see you down there."

"Drop your rifle," Fargo ordered. The man was too calm, and that worried him.

"Whatever you say, mister," Semple said, and let go. The rifle clattered at their feet and Semple raised his hands. "You caught me fair and square."

"Holler to your brother," Fargo said. "Tell him to throw down his pistol or I'll shoot you."

"You might as well go ahead," Semple said. "Hoby don't care a lick what happens to me. The only one Hoby cares about is Hoby."

"You're his brother."

"So? Kin doesn't mean no more to him than a stray dog. He tolerated Granger and me because we grew up together but that's all it was. You want him hollered at, you do it yourself."

"Fine," Fargo said, and cupped his other hand to his mouth. "Hoby Cotton! Do you hear me?"

A chortled ended with, "My ears work right fine. Which is more than I can say about your noggin. You should have lit a shuck while you could."

"I'm holding a six-gun on Semple," Fargo informed him. "Drop your hardware and follow my voice with your hands in the air and he gets to live."

"You must reckon I'm loco," Hoby replied.

"You don't care that I'll shoot him?"

"In the first place, I have to find new hard cases to ride with me anyhow, so what's one more? In the second place, you won't kill him in cold blood. You're not me. You don't have it in you."

"Told you," Semple Cotton said.

Hoby wasn't finished. "Fact is, I can go you one better. You hand your hardware to Semple and have him bring you here or I'll put a slug smack between my pa's eyes."

"He'll do it, too," Semple said.

"Shut the hell up." Fargo shifted and concentrated on the figure standing over the dead horse. He could try but he might miss.

"I won't wait all night," Hoby called out. "I can't risk my so-called pa dyin' on me from his crushed leg."

"His what?" Fargo said to Semple.

"The horse fell on it and pinned him. We can't see much but there's a heap of blood. It must be broke to pieces."

The marshal chose that moment to shout, "Fargo? Don't give in, you hear? He'll kill us whether you do or you don't give up your gun, so don't."

"I didn't ask for your two bits, Pa," Hoby said. "He doesn't do as I want, I'll deal with him and come back even madder."

"Do what you have to, you little wretch," Coltraine said. "I'm through kissin' your hind end."

"After all I've done for you, too."

Fargo had taken his eyes off Semple. A simple mistake, but he was holding a cocked Colt and doubted Semple would try anything. He was wrong.

Semple sprang and swatted at the Colt as Fargo brought it to bear, knocking it aside. It went off and Semple slammed into Fargo and both of them pitched to the grass.

Fargo kicked at Semple's head. He still had the Colt but a hand locked on his wrist to prevent him from using it. Another hand clamped onto his throat.

"Time for you to die," Semple snarled.

Fargo wrenched but Semple clung on. The fingers around his throat constricted. He grabbed Semple's wrist but couldn't budge it.

"You're not much," Semple hissed. "My grandma was stronger than you."

From the direction of the dead horse came an outcry and the boom of a shot.

Fargo had problems of his own. He exerted all his strength but Semple's fingers were steel. His breath was choked off and his lungs were starting to hurt from the lack of air.

Struggling fiercely, Fargo drove a fist into Semple's gut but all Semple did was grunt.

Spurs jangled, and Hoby Cotton bawled, "Out of the way, Semple. Give me a clear shot."

"Don't!" Semple shouted. "I almost have him."

The devil of it was, Semple was right. Fargo was beginning to black out. If he didn't break free he'd be strangled and if he did break free he'd be shot.

He did the only thing he could.

46

Fargo rammed his shoulder into Semple's chest, knocking Semple off his feet. In the same motion he swept Semple toward the sound of Hoby's voice. He felt the jolt of impact and Hoby squawked, and all three of them were down and in a tangle.

The grip on Fargo's neck slackened. Smashing his fist against Semple's forearm, Fargo broke free and rolled.

"Shoot him!" Semple bawled.

Not sure where Hoby was, and expecting to feel the searing impact of hot lead, Fargo lunged to his feet and ran.

"Get off me, damn you!" Hoby Cotton yelled.

Fargo went another dozen steps and flattened. Twisting his head, he could just make out the rising forms of the Cottons.

"He's gone, thanks to you," Hoby was saying. "I couldn't get a shot."

"Do we go after him?"

"In the dark?" Hoby replied. "Use your head and stay close."

They sprinted off.

Fargo didn't move. It might be another trick. Not until the drum of heavy hooves told him the Cottons were apparently skedaddling.

Rising, Fargo crept forward until he spied the bulk of the dead horse. "Coltraine?" he whispered.

There was no answer.

Fargo moved closer.

The lawman lay on his side with one arm bent unnaturally under him and his leg under the bay. His hat was missing and his holster was empty.

"Coltraine?" Fargo said again, and touched the lawman's shoulder.

Luther Coltraine opened his eyes and seemed to try to focus. "Fargo? That you? Did you get them?"

"They got away." Fargo saw that the front of the marshal's shirt was a lot darker than it should be. Blood, and a lot of it.

Coltraine coughed and dark specks flecked his lips and chin. "That's a shame. I hate to die with him still on the loose."

"He won't be for long," Fargo vowed.

Coltraine looked down at himself. "Part of me didn't think he'd do it. Not really. But he up and shot me with no more regret than if I was a fly."

Fargo remembered the bank teller and Rufus and all the others he had heard about. "The boy is a natural-born killer."

"How he could be mine, I'll never know," Coltraine said. "Sometimes I wonder if it wasn't me who sired him. If maybe she slept with someone else besides me."

Fargo hadn't thought of that. "Could be," he acknowledged.

"He's done me in," Coltraine said, and coughed some more.

"Anything I can do for you?"

"Don't go yet."

"I'll stay until . . ." Fargo didn't finish.

Coltraine gazed about them even though there was nothing to see. "Never reckoned it would be like this. By my own son, no less, if his ma's to be believed." He sighed. "Our pokes come back to haunt us when we least expect."

Fargo hoped not.

Coltraine bowed his head, and then said quietly, "I couldn't, when it came down to it."

"How's that again?"

"I couldn't shoot. I had my six-shooter out and pointin' right at him when he walked up but I couldn't squeeze the trigger. And do you know what he did? He laughed and kicked it out of my hand."

"He's lived too long," Fargo said. A strange thing to say about someone who hadn't seen eighteen summers.

"Did I ever tell you that Amanda is a she-cat under the sheet?"

"How did we get from him to her?"

"I don't want to die with him in my head." Coltraine sank back and closed his eyes. "It won't be long."

The wind picked up and stirred the dead horse's mane.

"I used to be one of the best lawmen around," Coltraine said wistfully. "Before that boy came along. Before he made my life hell."

Fargo realized he still held his Colt and holstered it.

"Funny thing is, there's not any pain. A slug in my chest and my leg half crushed and I don't feel much. How can that be?"

"You're lucky."

"You call this luck?" Coltraine said, and started to laugh but broke into another coughing fit. "I am bound for hell and that's for sure."

"If I had whiskey I'd offer you some."

"My saddlebag," Coltraine said. "There's a flask."

Fargo found it, a silver flask half-full. He opened it and pressed it to the lawman's good hand.

"I'm obliged." Coltraine swallowed and said, "Ahhh."

"Any kin you want to be told?" Fargo thought to ask.

"I wish there were. The only kin I have left in this world is that boy." Coltraine's mouth curled in a grim smile filled with blood. "Ain't that a hoot?"

"I'll give him your regards if I'm able when I do him in."

"You do that. You tell him that his pa . . ." Coltraine stopped and the flask fell from fingers gone limp and his chest deflated.

"Hell," Fargo said.

47

The Cottons had ridden all night and half of the next day and probably figured they were safe.

When Fargo saw the smoke he circled and came up on the woods from the south instead of the north. He tied the Ovaro to an oak and drew his Colt.

Ever since leaving Coltraine lying there in the dirt, he'd felt peculiar. As if part of him had become as hard as granite. He was filled with a fierce resolve, and he wouldn't be denied this side of the grave.

They were seated at their campfire, facing their back trail. They had coffee on, and Hoby was doing what he always did: laughing.

"Did you see the look on his face? It'll give me a grin the rest of my born days."

"Why do you suppose he didn't shoot?" Semple said. "He had the chance and didn't take it."

"Who knows? Stupid is as stupid does."

"What now?" Semple asked. "Stick around or go back to Texas or somethin' else?"

"How does Denver and the mountains thereabouts strike you?" Hoby said "I hear they're findin' silver and gold all over the place. They'd be more folks to rob than we can shake a stick at."

"We need some new gun hands," Semple suggested. "The two of us ain't hardly enough."

"What was it Ma used to say? Bad apples are easy to find. You just look under any big rock." Hoby laughed and bent for the coffeepot.

Fargo walked into the clearing. They didn't hear him and he went partway and stopped. "Sometimes you find bad apples sitting next to a fire."

The Cottons exploded to their feet and whirled, Hoby with a tin cup in his gun hand, Semple clawing to draw but he froze when he saw Fargo's Colt was already out and pointed.

"Well, now," Hoby said, grinning. "Ain't you the tricky cuss? You're startin' to take after me."

"We thought we'd lost you," Semple said.

"We have unfinished business, you gents and me," Fargo said. He locked eyes with Hoby. "Your pa said to give his regards. He took a while dying. They do that when they're lung shot."

"He deserved it," Hoby said. "I'd have made him suffer more if I'd had the time."

"You're a piece of work," Fargo said.

"I haven't heard that before." Hoby chuckled and casually tossed the tin cup to one side and raised his hands. "All right. You've caught us. Take us in."

"In?" Fargo said.

"To jail," Hoby said. "That's why my pa and you were after us. To arrest us so we'd be put on trial. That's how the law works."

"Do you see a badge on my buckskins?"

"None of the rest of the posse had tin stars, either. Just the marshal and the deputy."

"Hoby," Semple said. "That's not what he's sayin'."

For once the boy's quick wits were slow to savvy. "He got the drop on us, didn't he? Why else if not to take us in?"

"Is that what you think?" Fargo said, and twirled the Colt into his holster.

"What the blazes?" Hoby blurted. His surprise gave way to uncertainty and he looked at his brother.

"I told you," Semple said.

"I do declare," Hoby said. Grinning, he slowly lowered his arms and shifted his legs so he was poised on the balls of his feet. "If this don't beat all, mister. You should have just shot us."

"I want you to know it's coming," Fargo said.

"It could be we're better than you," Semple said. His fingers were splayed above his revolver and he flexed them. "It could be it's us that rides away."

"There's only one way to find out."

Hoby had absorbed the full import by now and was shaking his head in amusement. "Don't you beat all. There's not an hombre alive who can take both of us at the same time."

"Prove it," Fargo said.

Hoby tittered with glee. "I should thank you for givin' us peace of mind. I didn't like the notion of always havin' to look over my shoulder."

"Whenever you say to, little brother," Semple said.

"There's one thing first," Fargo said.

"Oh?" From Hoby.

"Your ma."

"What about her?"

"Was Coltraine the only gent she slept with?"

"What's it to you?" Hoby snapped.

"I'm curious, is all," Fargo said.

Hoby hesitated, then said, "My ma, bless her, trifled with every handsome galoot she set eyes on. Coltraine was but one of a whole wagonload of admirers."

"The marshal was right, then," Fargo said. "Then why try to ruin his life? Why follow him all the way from Texas when you couldn't be sure he was your real father?"

"I like playin' with folks. I like makin' 'em suffer. And he was the great Luther Coltraine. The tin star who could do no wrong. The man who couldn't be beat. Well, I beat him. I ran him out of Texas and I came here to toy with him some more and then kill him, and it was as fun as anything."

"All the misery you've caused."

"What you call misery I call a good laugh. And haven't you heard? Laughter is good for the soul."

Semple chuckled. "You sure are a hoot, Hoby. But shouldn't we get to it?"

"I reckon we should," Hoby said.

Fargo was as ready as he'd ever be. "Whenever you want to die."

Hoby grinned. "After we're done with you I might just go back to that two-bit town and help myself to that Brenner gal. Maybe cart her around with us and let her do the cookin' and poke her every night. Semple and me both."

"I'd like that," Semple said.

Fargo waited, motionless.

"Nothin' more to say?" Hoby taunted. He gazed at the sky and at the woods and at his brother and back at Fargo. "Me either."

"Now?" Semple said.

"Now," Hoby said.

Their hands flashed, and so did Fargo's. He drew and fanned a shot into Hoby Cotton and shifted and fanned another into Semple before either cleared leather. Hoby was jolted back but Semple barely flinched and fired but in his haste he missed. Fargo fanned again, his Colt cracking and bucking. The slug caught Semple Cotton in the mouth and pulped his lower lip even as it shattered his teeth and cored through his skull and burst out the back of his head.

Hoby fanned a shot of his own and Fargo felt pain in his shoulder. He aimed and shot Hoby in the chest and Hoby staggered and sent a slug whizzing under his arm.

Fargo shot Hoby as he raised his revolver, shot him as his legs buckled, shot him as he keeled to the ground.

Fargo walked over and put his boot on Hoby's six-shooter as Hoby tried to lift it. His own Colt was empty and he commenced to reload.

Hoby Cotton grinned. "You've done shot me to ribbons."

"You're not dead yet," Fargo said, inserting a second cartridge.

"Lordy, I hurt," Hoby said, and grimaced. "You could have blown my brains out like you did Semple's but you didn't. Folks say I'm snake-mean but you're just as mean as me."

"I have my moments," Fargo said, sliding a fourth cartridge into the chamber.

"I've had mine. And you know what? I wouldn't have done any of it different. All I've ever wanted was to have fun."

"All I want," Fargo said, sliding a fifth cartridge in, and then cocking the Colt, "is this." He pointed and fired.

LOOKING FORWARD!
The following is the opening
section of the next novel in the exciting
Trailsman series from Signet:

TRAILSMAN #390
DEVIL'S DEN

Devil's Den, Northwest Arkansas, 1860—where Fargo locks
horns with a pack of savage killers in a deadly corner
of Ozark country.

Fargo hadn't intended to knock Deputy Sheriff Harney Roscoe through the wall of the Hog's Breath saloon. It just happened to be a thin wall and a solid haymaker.

Wood cracked, splinters flew, and Roscoe did a backward Virginia reel, stumbling across the boardwalk and landing flat on his back in the wagon-rutted main street of Busted Flush, Arkansas.

Fargo stepped through the newly created exit just as Roscoe, his pasty face swollen and bleeding, slapped at his holster.

Fargo's walnut-gripped Colt formed a blur from holster to hand.

"If you even *sneeze*," Fargo warned in a deceptively soft tone, "you'll never hear the gesundheit."

A menacing, metallic click sounded on Fargo's left.

"All right, Skye," said an amiable voice, "toss that lead-chucker down."

Fargo did as ordered and glanced to his left. Sheriff Dub Gillycuddy, a big Colt's Dragoon filling his hand, stood grinning at him.

"Trailsman," he said, leathering the big gun, "most jaspers are content to just raise hell—you always have to *tilt* it a few inches. All right, what's the larceny this time?"

"Hell, I didn't start it, Dub. I was in a friendly game of pasteboards when Roscoe here horned in and declared table stakes. When I told him it was strictly a two-dollar limit, he took exception."

"Uh-huh. And who tossed the first punch?"

"Well," Fargo admitted, "that would be me. But only after Deputy Roscoe tried to jerk me outta my chair."

The sheriff glanced at his vanquished deputy. "Is that the straight, Harney?"

But just then Roscoe made a sucking noise like a plugged drain and passed out.

Sheriff Gillycuddy studied his badly mauled deputy for a few moments, noting the split and swelling lips, bloodied nose, and blue-black left eye already puffing up like a hot biscuit.

"Hell's fire, Fargo! If you'd beat on him any longer, I'd have to pick him up with a blotter."

"The son of a bitch bit me, Dub. I can't abide that in a sporting fight, not from a man."

A portly, balding man in a filthy apron stepped through the hole in the wall. "Sheriff, *look* at what Fargo done to my place!"

"Actually," Fargo pointed out, "it was Roscoe who went through the wall."

"At the end of *your* fist! Somebody owes me—"

Gillycuddy raised a hand to silence the sputtering barkeep. The sheriff was a handsome, avuncular man in his early fifties whose easygoing manner and broad-minded tolerance kept getting him elected although the law-and-order faction wondered how his monthly rent could be twice his salary.

"Just hold your horses, Silas. Who started this catawampus?"

"I can't rightly say. But Fargo seemed peaceful enough before Harney showed up."

The sheriff cast another glance toward his supine deputy. "Hell, there ain't nothing but bone twixt his jug handles and he's always on the scrap. I'll 'low as how it wasn't likely you, Skye, who started the dustup. But I couldn't just let you shoot my deputy. He's also the town dogcatcher and hog reeve."

"But my wall!" Silas protested. "That hole—"

"The town fund will pay for it," Gillycuddy cut him off. "Skye, I'm gonna have to toss you in the pokey for one night. And there'll be a five-dollar fine for disturbing the peace. Here, lend a hand. . . ."

Fargo and the sheriff dragged Roscoe up onto the relative safety of the boardwalk. As the two men crossed the wide street toward the jailhouse Fargo spoke up.

"Dub, I don't mind a night in the calaboose. But as to that five-dollar fine . . . there's a reason I was playing a limit game."

"Light in the pockets, huh? Sorry, old son. If you can't post the pony, it's a dollar a day in jail."

Fargo shrugged. The tall, broad-shouldered, slim-hipped frontiersman was clad in fringed buckskins and wore a dusty white hat with a bullet hole in the crown. A close-cropped beard and lake-blue eyes set off his weather-bronzed face.

"Is the food any better," he asked, "since last time you jugged me?"

"The eats are tolerable if you pick the weevils out. But I only got the one cell, and I'm 'fraid you're gonna have to share it with the most foul-tempered Injin I ever met up with."

"What tribe?"

"Ahh, I b'lieve he's a half-breed Choctaw. That red son smells like a bear's cave."

"Jumped the rez?" Fargo meant the sprawling Indian Territory that began only about ten miles west of this rugged corner of the Ozark region.

"I s'pose, but his English is mighty good—or at least his cussin' is. I'm about to shoot that hot-jawing son of a buck. Won't give me his name, but he don't hesitate to give me the rough side of his tongue."

The sheriff suddenly laughed. "Why, that blanket ass is plumb loco. His damn saddlebags was stuffed with tossed-out envelopes he took when the post office took out their trash. Won't tell me why."

Fargo's growing nubbin of suspicion hardened into a certainty. "Now this Choctaw . . . is he heavyset with a string of bright-painted magic pebbles around his neck?"

Gillycuddy's head snapped toward Fargo. "You know him?"

"He goes by the name of Cranky Man. He saved my life once a few miles from here near Lead Hill."

"Cranky Man, huh? Well, mister, he is that. I mighta guessed you'd be chummy with a reprobate like him. The hell's he want with all them envelopes?"

"He can't read so he thinks there's big magic in white man's handwriting. First time I ever saw him he was stealing old army contracts from one of my saddle pockets."

"Yeah? Well, that Indian wasn't born—he was squeezed out of a bar rag. When I arrested him he was drunker'n the lords of Creation. All he's done since, when he ain't cussin' me out, is demand liquor. Claims his religion requires him to drink."

Gillycuddy pulled up in front of the jailhouse door. "Le'me have that toothpick in your boot. And where's your Henry?"

"Locked up at Drake's livery," Fargo replied, reluctantly surrendering his Arkansas toothpick. "I want a chit for these weapons."

The sheriff grunted and led the way into a cubbyhole office with wanted dodgers plastered to the walls and a battered kneehole desk. Fargo immediately spotted Cranky Man in the cramped cell, sitting on one of two army cots and picking his teeth with a match. He saw Fargo and did a double take.

"Skye Fargo! Hell, I figured you were pegged out by now."

"Sorry to disappoint you. Last time I saw you, you said you were headed back to Mississippi."

"I say a lot of things I don't do." Cranky Man aimed a malevolent glance at the sheriff. "Won't matter now. If these peckerwoods have their way, I'm gonna be the guest of honor at a hemp social."

Gillycuddy stuffed Fargo's knife and gun in a drawer and banged it shut. "That's a lie on stilts, savage. I'm holding you until a tumbleweed wagon rolls through town and hauls your worthless, flea-bit ass back to the Nations where Andy Jackson, in his infinite wisdom, sent you."

"Fuck him and fuck you, starman," the Choctaw shot back. "You and your whole cockeyed town can kiss my red ass."

Fargo bit back a grin as he watched the sheriff's normally mellow features suffuse with purple anger.

"You just keep pushing me, chief. You couldn't lick snot off your upper lip, so don't be playing top dog around me."

"Who'd you kill?" Cranky Man asked Fargo when the sheriff admitted him to the cell.

"A little misunderstanding with a deputy," Fargo replied, sitting on the empty cot.

The Choctaw had clearly fallen on hard times. Beggar's-lice leaped from his clothing, and the weathered grooves of his face had deepened. His beaded moccasins were frayed and torn, and some of the beadwork was missing from his deerskin shirt.

"Got any Indian burner?" Cranky Man asked hopefully.

"Nope."

Cranky Man swore. "What I wouldn't give right now to be a fish in an ocean of whiskey."

A buckboard rattled to a stop outside and Sheriff Gillycuddy glanced out the window. If a voice could frown, his did now. "Stand by for a blast. Here comes Marcella and Malinda Scott."

Fargo perked up at the mention of females. "Sisters or mother and daughter?"

"Sisters, and they're both lookers. They moved here from someplace in Ohio to take over the Ozark West Transfer Line. This was after old Tubby Scott, their uncle, turned up dead. He left the business to them, but all they've done is bollix it up but good. It ain't no job for calicos."

"Tubby Scott," Fargo repeated. "Yeah, I recall hearing about him—Orrin Scott. Made his pile hauling mail and freight between Fayetteville and Van Buren."

The sheriff nodded. "Until he was found dead one morning in the crapper behind the station house. His neck was snapped so hard his head flopped around like it was attached to a rubber tether."

The door swung open to admit the prettiest whirling dervish Fargo had seen in some time. She flounced toward Gillycuddy's desk in a froufrou of rustling skirts.

"Sheriff," she demanded, "*what* are you going to do about Anslowe Deacon?"

Gillycuddy raised both hands like a priest blessing his flock. "Sheathe your horns, lady. You're pretty as a speckled pony, Miss Marcella, but you always rare up like a she-grizz with cubs."

Fargo sized up Marcella Scott with appreciative eyes. She had a startlingly pretty oval face with a high-bridged nose and green eyes blazing with indignation. Strawberry-blond hair framed her face in a mass of ringlets.

"How pretty I am is nothing to the matter! If I were a man you'd take me more seriously!"

The sheriff shrugged indifferently. "No need to be so snippety.

It ain't my fault if Deacon runs a better short line than you do. That's competition for you."

"Competition? The man is a murdering criminal!"

The door opened again and a second breathtaking beauty— Malinda Scott, Fargo assumed—glided in much more demurely. She was shapely and petite with sun-streaked auburn hair barely controlled by tortoiseshell combs. Her lacquered straw hat featured a brightly dyed ostrich feather and gay "follow me lads" ribbons.

"Well, now, as to *criminals*," the sheriff told Marcella, "you're the one who's out of jail on bail, not Deacon. And bail can be revoked easy in Fayetteville."

"I did *not* steal Truella Brubaker's bracelet! I told you it was among the items taken from a locked desk in the station office— yet another crime you've done nothing about."

Malinda, who hadn't spoken a word yet, spotted Fargo and gave him a wide smile that threatened to crack her rosy cheeks.

"Yeah, well, I told you that's Fayetteville jurisdiction. And about them stolen items—there was something else besides that bracelet that you're agitated as all get-out about, Miss Marcella. Why'n't you put your cards on the table? I will help you, but I have to know what I'm looking for."

Fargo watched the imperious beauty blush. "Never mind that. Anslowe Deacon is a vicious criminal and you know it! You just lack the will and courage to do anything about it."

Gillycuddy let out a weary sigh and caught Fargo's eye. "You know, Trailsman, like they say—a pretty girl is a malady."

For the first time Marcella noticed Fargo with frowning disapproval. "The Trailsman? I've heard my workers mention that name. Are you Skye Fargo?"

"I am in this case," Fargo assured her, doffing his hat.

"And a criminal, I see."

"Oh, he's more or less law-abiding until he goes off on a bust," the sheriff vouchsafed. "I've never locked him up for anything worse than brawling. And once for—ahh—violating the Sunday blue laws."

"What you mean is that he fornicated on the Sabbath?"

"I wasn't Bible raised," Fargo offered in his own defense.

"Look at it this way, lady," Cranky Man piped up. "Every time you whiteskins break one of them Ten Commandments of yours, you still got nine left."

"Yes, well I'm sure you two ruffians manage to break all ten in one day."

"Usually by noon," Fargo assured her.

Marcella studied Fargo in silence for perhaps ten seconds. "Well, right now I *need* a ruffian. Are you interested in a job?"

"Oh, let's *do* hire him, Sis," Malinda spoke up in a lilting, musical voice she must have worked on. "He's the most handsome, rugged man I've ever seen."

"You'll have to forgive my sister, Fargo," Marcella said, anger spiking her voice. "I won't call her a painted cat, but only because she doesn't charge money."

"Do tell?" Fargo said, raking his eyes over the comely lass.

"If I was paid what I'm worth," Malinda put in to spite her sister, "I'd be richer than the Queen of Sheba."

"Well, now," Fargo said, "what a delightful girl."

Cranky Man snorted and Marcella slapped her sister. Malinda smiled at Fargo.

"Fargo, you best con this over good," the sheriff warned. "There's considerable stink brewing around here, all right, and it ain't all blowing off that Choctaw. I know how you are about women, but these two pert skirts will get you killed."

The acid-tongued Marcella whirled on the lawman. "Nobody asked you, buttinsky! If you'd do your job I wouldn't need to hire someone."

"I'll take the job," Fargo told her, "whatever it is. But only if you hire on Cranky Man here, too. He's not as worthless as he looks."

"I'm desperate," Marcella admitted.

"How 'bout it, Dub?" Fargo asked the sheriff. "Will you spring us?"

Gillycuddy pushed to his feet and snatched the cell key from a wall peg. "This time you get the breaks, Fargo. I'll even drop the fine. These gals could use your help, all right. 'Sides, I'm glad to get shut of this stinking savage. But *don't* go killing every living thing you see. I can only ignore so much, and if the hotheads around here get too riled up, all three of us could end up doing a dance on nothing."

He clanged the door open, then looked at Marcella. "Why are you ladies here, anyhow? Just to aggravate my ulcers?"

Marcella's pretty face turned grim. "I saved that for last. Please come outside."

All three men trooped out behind the women. Marcella pulled out the pin to drop the tailgate of the buckboard.

The sheriff's face turned fish-belly white. "K. T. Christ!"

The dead man lying inside, glazed eyes staring wide open at nothing, was missing at least a fifth of his head.

No other series packs this much heat!

THE TRAILSMAN

Follow the trail of Penguin's Action Westerns at
penguin.com/actionwesterns

THE LAST OUTLAWS
The Lives and Legends of Butch Cassidy and the Sundance Kid

by Thom Hatch

Butch Cassidy and the Sundance Kid are two of the most celebrated figures of American lore. As leaders of the Wild Bunch, also known as the Hole-in-the-Wall Gang, they planned and executed the most daring bank and train robberies of the day, with an uprecedented professionalism.

The Last Outlaws brilliantly brings to life these thrilling, larger-than-life personalities like never before, placing the legend of Butch and Sundance in the context of a changing—and shrinking—American West, as the rise of 20th century technology brought an end to a remarkable era. Drawing on a wealth of fresh research, Thom Hatch pushes aside the myth and offers up a compelling, fresh look at these icons of the Wild West.

National bestselling author
RALPH COMPTON

"A writer in the tradition of Louis L'Amour and Zane Grey!" —*Huntsville Times*

Available wherever books are sold or at
penguin.com

S543